GHOST TRACKERS

The Unreal World of Ghosts, Ghost-Hunting, and the Paranormal

By Chris Gudgeon

Foreword by Joe MacLeod,
host of TV's hit series *Ghost Trackers*

TUNDRA BOOKS

To Charlie, Tavish, Keating, Hannah, Nathanial, Madison, Carson, Duncan, Griffin, and all the Ghost Trackers *fans around the world.*

Text copyright © 2010 by Chris Gudgeon

Published in Canada by Tundra Books,
75 Sherbourne Street, Toronto, Ontario M5A 2P9

Published in the United States by Tundra Books of Northern New York,
P.O. Box 1030, Plattsburgh, New York 12901

Library of Congress Control Number: 2009938451

Library and Archives Canada Cataloguing in Publication

Gudgeon, Chris, 1959-
    Ghost trackers : the unreal world of ghosts, ghost-hunting,
and the paranormal / Chris Gudgeon.

ISBN 978-0-88776-950-4

    1. Ghosts--Juvenile literature.
2. Parapsychology--Juvenile literature. I. Title.
BF1461.G83 2010   j133.1   C2009-906019-1

We acknowledge the financial support of the Government of Canada through the Book Publishing Industry Development Program (BPIDP) and that of the Government of Ontario through the Ontario Media Development Corporation's Ontario Book Initiative. We further acknowledge the support of the Canada Council for the Arts and the Ontario Arts Council for our publishing program.

ONTARIO ARTS COUNCIL
CONSEIL DES ARTS DE L'ONTARIO

Published in cooperation with CCI Entertainment Ltd.

Design: Paul Dotey

Printed and bound in Canada

1 2 3 4 5 6   15 14 13 12 11 10

CONTENTS

If from antiquity to the present, and since the beginning of man, there are men who have seen the bodies of ghosts and spirits and heard their voices, how can we say that they do not exist?

– Chinese philosopher Mo Tzu,
who lived from 470 to 391 BCE.

GHOST TRACKERS WANTED, NO EXPERIENCE REQUIRED

Foreword by Joe Macleod, host of TV's *Ghost Trackers*

Ghosts.

Haunted houses.

Spirit voices.

Poltergeists.

Are they evidence of life after death? Portals to an alternate universe? Or are they a natural occurrence we've yet to understand? Somewhere between science and fantasy is the realm of the paranormal.

Welcome to the world of Ghost Trackers, where kids just like you are interested in ghosts and the paranormal. Are ghosts real? Can a house be haunted? Are those strange sounds at night just your imagination playing tricks? These are questions that every kid asks – and Ghost Trackers try to answer.

How do you become a Ghost Tracker? All you need is an open mind, an interest in ghosts, and a desire to investigate the unexplained.

Some people say that ghosts don't exist. Some just aren't sure. But lots and lots of people have seen and heard things they can't explain. It's likely that even you or someone in your family has had an encounter with the paranormal.

This book is for fans of the TV show . . . and for anybody who has ever wondered about the truth behind all those ghost stories. It's a book for true believers and skeptics alike, and it's a book for kids like you, who are brave enough to explore the world of the unknown.

Happy haunting!

Joe Macleod

www.ghosttrackers.tv

INTRODUCTION
Do You Believe in Ghosts?

EVERY HALLOWEEN IN MY HOMETOWN, people head down to an old graveyard near the outskirts of town. It's one of the most historic – and creepiest – places around. Some of the graves date back over one hundred and fifty years. There are ancient, cracked headstones covered in moss, the names and dates faded. There are old stone crosses and a large marble angel, her

wings chipped and worn on the edges.

On any given night, you might find a handful of people skulking quietly through the spooky graveyard. But on October 31, things get busy, with kids, parents, teenagers, and even grandmas wearing heavy winter coats to ward off the cold night air – every age and kind of person you can imagine. And they are all there for one reason: ghosts.

You see, this cemetery is rumored to be the most haunted place in the area. There are at least five resident spirits, including a gold miner murdered for his secret hoard, a widow in a black shroud who is still searching for her husband lost at sea

Are You a Believer?

A recent study by the Gallup Poll asked people to pick which paranormal activities they believed in. Below are the top five answers. What would be on your top-five list?

1. ESP (extrasensory perception)
2. Haunted houses
3. Ghostly visitations
4. Mind reading
5. Seeing into the future

a century ago, and a lonely little boy who is forever looking for someone to play with in his ghost world.

Why the fuss on Halloween? That's the night the ghosts seem to be the
most active. And everyone has the same goal. They want to see a ghost.
They want to find out if ghosts are real.

Ghosts, it seems, are on everyone's mind. A recent poll by CBS News
found that almost half of all American adults believe in ghosts. And the
same study concluded that almost a quarter of adults have actually seen one.

For me, I have always been a little doubtful. I had seen and heard some
strange things when I was a kid – phantom footsteps in the middle of the
night, odd lights and faces in the dark. But once I became an adult, I
decided those weird things were all just my imagination playing tricks.

But then one night something happened to me that changed my mind.
I was staying over at my friends' house. They lived in a very old home in
the country that had once served as an inn for weary travelers. My wife
and I had heard the stories of the ghosts that supposedly haunted the
place, but we thought nothing of them. On this particular night, my wife
and I were sound asleep in the guest bedroom when we both suddenly
woke up. I had a strange feeling, like something weird was going on, but
I didn't know what.

That's when I noticed a strange luminous shape, vaguely human, at
the foot of the bed. At first I thought it was a reflection of some kind,
maybe from a car's headlights from the road nearby. But the pale light
did not go away. It just sort of floated. I thought that maybe it was my
imagination. Remember, I was still half-asleep. But then my wife asked,
"Do you see that?"

Voices From the Past

"It is wonderful that five thousand years have now elapsed since the creation of the world, and still it is undecided whether or not there has ever been an instance of the spirit of any person appearing after death. All argument is against it; but all belief is for it."

– British writer Samuel Johnson, who lived from 1709 to 1784.

She saw the same strange shape I did, which meant it couldn't all be in my head. We lay silently in the dark room for a few moments until we realized that the shape was gone. We slept with the light on for the rest of the night.

Was it a ghost? I don't know for sure. But I know I definitely saw something that I couldn't explain.

This unreal encounter got me interested in ghosts and the paranormal. I began doing my own research, reading books about ghosts, and interviewing scientists and professional ghost hunters. Finally, I created a TV series called *Ghost Trackers*. It's a reality show where we work with regular kids like you, teach them proper ghost-hunting techniques, and put them in a real haunted house. Guided by an experienced ghost hunter, our Ghost Trackers conduct an investigation to find out if the house is really haunted and to help answer the question: Do ghosts really exist?

I still don't know the answer. But since I've started to take a closer look, I know that I've seen and heard a lot of weird things that I can't easily comprehend. Sometimes they've been small things, like the time we were taping *Ghost Trackers* at an old farmhouse. Every time I came out of the building from helping to set things up, I noticed that my watch had stopped.

And there have been big things too. Like a door closing right behind one of the Ghost Trackers when there was no wind to push it or anyone else in the house to move it.

We got that one on film. Or the time when we were about to shoot footage at an old inn where two children had died almost one hundred years ago. We'd heard stories of ghostly children running and playing in the halls and of the repeated sightings of an old woman carrying a baby. Just before our first Ghost Tracker went into the inn to start her investigation, as the crew and fans of the show stood outside in the cold night air, an unmistakable sound came from inside the building.

It was a baby crying.

Most of us heard it and looked at each other in shock. We knew the inn was empty; we'd finished carefully checking it minutes before. And with remote-control cameras set up throughout the house to follow our Ghost Trackers' investigation, we knew that it was impossible for anyone to have snuck in.

What do I make of these otherworldly encounters? All I know is that I am sure there is something unusual going on. Whether it's the spirits of the dead who have come back to communicate with the living, some kind of unknown electrical force at work, or anything in between, I just can't say.

Haunted Links

Want to see some of the eerie action from the hit TV series *Ghost Trackers*? Check out the Freaky Findings videos on the show's Web site! www.ghosttrackers.tv

But we can ask questions, investigate, and explore. And that's what *Ghost Trackers: The Unreal World of Ghosts, Ghost-Hunting, and the Paranormal* is all about. It's a book for anyone who's ever wondered: Are ghosts for real or is my mind just playing tricks on me? We cover everything, from the history of ghosts to an overview of scientific research into the paranormal, with special chapters on the nature of ghosts and haunted houses. Finally, we put it all together and help you get ready to start your own Ghost Tracker investigations. Of course, there'll be a true ghost story or two along the way! Who knows? Maybe one day, one of you reading this book will uncover the truth.

1. A HISTORY OF GHOSTLY MYSTERIES
Ghosts Throughout the Ages

ARE GHOSTS FOR REAL? It's a question that people have been asking for thousands of years.

Every ancient culture passed down stories and myths about mysterious ghosts and spirits, and it's amazing how, over centuries and centuries, the stories have not changed that much.

Here's one that could be from the latest scary video you rented. Late at night, a man is woken up in his bed by the sound of a ghost howling and rattling the chains that are wrapped around its body. The ghost confronts the man and leads him outside to the yard. There, the ghost points to a spot on the ground, then slowly fades.

The next day, the man, still terrified, digs in the exact spot where the ghost had pointed. Buried deep in the dirt, the man finds a skeleton wrapped in chains, a victim of some long-forgotten murder.

This is apparently a true story, and it was recorded by a respected historian named Pliny the Younger almost two thousand years ago.

Pliny's isn't the first ghost story in history. For as long as people have been keeping records, they have been writing about ghosts. Six thousand years ago, the Egyptians wrote about *ka*, a spirit that lived inside the body. According to hieroglyphics (picture writing found on the walls of pyramids and other ancient Egyptian ruins), the ka left a person's body when he or she died. It would stay near the corpse to protect it. Priests had to perform special rituals to feed and take care of the ka or it would leave the corpse and begin to haunt the living.

The Greeks and Romans had a slightly different take on the dearly departed. They believed that the spirits of the dead left the body and went to a special world. In Greek mythology, that world was called Hades, a dark and misty place where spirits spent eternity. Under special circumstances, these spirits could leave the underworld and come back to earth. This usually happened when they had a job to do, like deliver an important message, and often the spirits would appear to living friends and family members through dreams. Pliny's father (known as Pliny the Elder) told the tale of how the ghost of a famous warrior visited him and commanded him to write the story of a great battle. When Pliny woke up the next day, he started work on the *History of the Germanic Wars*, which is considered today to be one of the first real history books ever written.

Even back then there were skeptics. Many questioned whether ghosts were real or imaginary. "It has been maintained that no man in his senses ever saw a ghost," wrote the Roman historian Plutarch in the first century CE. In his day, many people believed that reports of ghost sightings were usually the imaginary visions of "women and children, or of men whose intellects are impaired by some physical infirmity."

But Plutarch wasn't a skeptic himself. He recounts a ghost story in his biography of Marcus Brutus, a man famous for having helped kill the Roman general Julius Caesar. According to Plutarch, Brutus once told his friends that he had been visited by a frightening specter that warned him that the end was near. The visitation upset Brutus a lot, and he did, in fact, die a short time later.

Plutarch also told a story about a man named Damon who was murdered in the local baths – a kind of Roman version of a public hot tub. After the murder, strange things started happening at the baths. People would hear ghostly groaning in the middle of the night and see spectral shadows on the wall. Eventually, the building was boarded up. "To this very day," Plutarch wrote in his *Parallel Lives*, "those who live in the neighbourhood imagine that they see strange sights and are terrified with cries of sorrow."

What Homer Said

Before the TV show *The Simpsons* was created, the most famous Homer was a blind poet who lived almost three thousand years ago. He wrote two famous epics, long poems that tell the story of legendary heroes. The excerpt below is from Homer's *Iliad*. It tells of a meeting between the poem's hero, the warrior Achilles, and the ghost of his dead friend. It's one of the first ghost stories ever told.

"You sleep, Achilles, and have forgotten me; you loved me living, but now that I am dead you think of me no further. Bury me with all speed that I may pass the gates of Hades."

THE DARK SIDE OF THE DARK AGES

After the end of the Roman Empire and before the rise of powerful European states is a period of time that historians call the Middle Ages, or the Dark Ages. They were referred to as "dark" not because the sun wasn't shining but because there was a lot of hunger, war, and disease. Few people lived past the age of forty.

It would have been great to be a Ghost Tracker back in the Dark Ages. It was a time of witches and pagan rituals, when wizardry was considered an honest profession, and when stories of ghosts were commonplace.

Since most people could not read or write, a lot of the stories have been lost over time. But some have been passed down. One of the best-known tales concerns a famous spirit known as the Ghost of Beaucaire, named after the village in France where it appeared.

The ghost was believed to be the spirit of a young man named Guilhem — William, in modern English — who was killed in a street fight. A week after his death, the ghost began visiting the home of his cousin, an eleven-year-old girl named Marie. At first, she was afraid. But after a while, Marie realized that the ghost was only trying to communicate with her. Over the following weeks, the ghost visited Marie more than ten times, and soon news of the ghostly visitations spread. Friends, family members, and neighbors came by to talk to Guilhem through Marie, and Guilhem was happy to answer all their questions about life in the afterworld.

This story is interesting to Ghost Trackers like us because it shows that hauntings have changed little over the centuries. Guilhem died a violent death, and ghosts (for reasons researchers don't yet understand) are often the spirits of people who died under tragic circumstances. Also, Guilhem appeared to his eleven-year-old cousin. As any paranormal researcher will tell you, kids are much better at ghost-hunting than adults — maybe because they have a keener sixth sense or are more open-minded.

One more thing. The story of Guilhem and Marie is one of the earliest well-documented accounts of a ghost communicating to people through a medium (a term for a person who is a contact point between our world and the realm of spirits). Often a spirit will talk to people indirectly through

Why Are So Many Castles Haunted?

The Dark Ages lasted from about 600 CE to about 1000 CE. It was a time of knights, feudal lords, and castles. Many of these castles still stand to this day, and they are among the most haunted sites in the world.

Why are they so haunted? There are a couple of theories.

First, castles often included underground jail cells and torture chambers, scenes of slow, painful deaths and murderous attacks. Ghost hunters believe that ghosts are often the spirits of people who died suddenly or in an unpleasant way.

Second, castles are very, very old, and old places, for whatever reason, seem to collect ghosts.

There is also a third, more curious theory. Some researchers believe that the more solid a substance is, the more attractive it is to ghostly energy. Castles are often made of cut rocks or stones, so these could literally act like magnets for ghosts. (See the section on the Stone Tape Theory in Chapter 2.)

So far, there is no evidence to prove any of these theories. But one thing is for certain: When it comes to Ghost Tracking, castles can't be beat.

a medium. In Guilhem's case, while several people saw his ghost, he only spoke through Marie. Talk about putting words in someone's mouth!

Of course, there's a chance Marie was just tricking people by speaking in a funny voice and pretending to say things she thought Guilhem would say. But since there were no Ghost Trackers around back then to investigate the story, we may never know the truth.

In any case, as we will soon see, mediums like Marie would later play an important role in the history of ghosts, and they helped trigger a movement that led to a more scientific approach to studying ghosts, ghost-hunting, and the paranormal.

THE REBIRTH OF GHOUL

One of the most important changes during the Dark Ages was the rise of organized religion throughout the world. Before these troubled times, the Roman Empire had been the most influential force in Europe, helping to bring law and order to many remote places. Slowly though, Christianity grew in popularity, and it became a new organizing power.

At the same time, some cities and countries were becoming stronger and wealthier. The invention of the printing press, a greater focus on educating children, and the rise of universities – all these important things were happening at once. Eventually, the Dark Ages gave way to a new era of exploration, science, and learning known as the Renaissance (which means "rebirth"). It was called that because people believed they were witnessing the rebirth of civilization.

Still, ghosts and paranormal phenomena continued to be reported. The difference was that, rather than just accepting the fact that the spirits of the dead walked the earth, people tried to understand what was going on.

One of the first was a man named Lewes Lavater, a Swiss priest. In

One computer artist's impression of the devil.

1572, he wrote *Of Ghostes and Spirites walking by nyght*, the first serious book about ghosts ever written. He classified more than a dozen different kinds of ghosts and spirits, and he developed theories that kept with the religious attitudes of the time. He believed that good ghosts, the ones that came to comfort the living, were sent by God. Bad ghosts, the ones that frightened people, were sent by the devil.

Lavater's book is just one example of how the attitude toward the paranormal was changing, with people taking a more scientific approach to ghosts. The King of

England wrote a serious book on the subject around the same time. James I had a passion for studying the paranormal, and his paper/book was called *Daemonologie*. In James's mind, ghosts were the work of witches and Satan. (James thought that the devil himself was a spirit.) He believed that God had special rules for the dead, one being that "the soule once parting from the bodie, cannot wander anie longer in the worlde, but to the owne resting place must it goe immediatelie."

James's book was a scholarly work, and not widely read. So even though many of the king's subjects shared his belief that ghosts were a kind of demon, most people considered ghosts to be spirits of the dead, returned to earth to complete some unfinished business, as the famous story of the Cock Lane Ghost shows us.

The year was 1762, and late one night, twelve-year-old Betty Parsons was sharing a bed with an older family friend named Fanny Kent. Betty and her family lived in a house in London, England, on a street named Cock Lane.

Betty heard a weird scratching sound on her wall and reported the account to her father, William. She was very frightened, and she believed the strange scraping noise was a ghost foretelling her own death.

Weeks later, Fanny died suddenly.

Fanny's husband said it was smallpox, a common, often deadly disease back then. But a little while later, the scratching noises returned. The ghost was back, and this time it told an incredible story. Fanny hadn't died from smallpox after all; she had been murdered by her husband!

The ghost supposedly communicated by rapping on the wall, using a series of knocking combinations, and soon people were flocking to the Parsons's house – and paying an admission price – to hear the ghostly knocking. Angered by the ghost's story, they demanded that Fanny's husband be tried for murder.

The case was investigated by several people, including Dr. Samuel Johnson, one of England's most famous writers. He agreed to meet the ghost at the site of Fanny's tomb, but when the ghost never showed up, Johnson declared that Betty and her father were making the whole thing up.

The two were arrested for the fraud, and while Betty was set free, William went to jail for five years.

Despite the ruling, many Londoners believed the story and felt that Betty and her father were innocent. Today, it's impossible to find the truth. But there is one interesting footnote. Years later, workmen were digging in the basement of the Parsons' house when they came upon a gruesome site. It was the skeleton of a woman who would have been roughly Fanny's age when she died. Strange coincidence or proof that the Cock Lane Ghost was for real?

The answer is lost in the mists of time.

MEDIUMS, WELL DONE

The Fox sisters: Maggie left, Katy center, and their older sister, Leah

People have always been interested in ghosts. But the scientific study of the paranormal didn't begin until the 1800s, initiated by strange circumstances surrounding two sisters. The year was 1847, and Maggie and Katy Fox had just moved into a new house with their parents. Within a few days, the sisters started hearing odd noises in the middle of the night: banging that seemed to come from behind the kitchen cabinet and what sounded like ghostly footsteps shuffling up stairs. Frightened, they ran to their parents, who were in their own bedroom and had heard the noises as well.

Over the next few nights, the noises continued. And then something even stranger happened.

The ghost, it seemed, began to communicate with the girls.

"Mr. Splitfoot," Katy said, using the nickname the girls had come up with for the strange, shuffling spirit, "do as I do."

Katy clapped her hands four times and, to everyone's amazement, they heard the ghost reply with four knocks.

They quickly came up with a simple code, similar to the one used by the Cock Lane Ghost: one knock for *yes*, two knocks for *no*. The girls' mother, who was probably more frightened than they were, asked the ghost a series of questions. The family soon pieced together the phantom's story. His name was Charlie Rosna, and in life he had been a peddler, a kind of old-fashioned door-to-door salesman. He'd gone missing six years earlier – murdered, it seems – and his body was buried in the Fox family's cellar.

Word of the Fox resident ghost spread quickly, and soon people were coming from miles around to hear the wondrous rapping and to communicate with Charlie's ghost. The news also seemed to get around the spirit realm as well, and it wasn't long before other ghosts were calling on the Fox sisters. Because of their ability to communicate with spirits, Maggie and Katy were soon identified as mediums, and they quickly became a pop sensation, giving demonstrations of their powers across the United States.

People paid money to see their public séances, which soon went beyond simple spirit knocking to include doors opening, tables rising into the air of their own accord, and other freaky phenomena. Was it all a hoax? Some believed that it was. But others were convinced the sisters were really communicating with spirits, and over the course of hundreds of public séances, no one ever caught the Fox sisters cheating. Horace Greeley, editor of the *New York Tribune*, one of the most important newspapers of the time, went to several of Maggie and Katy's séances and concluded that they were for real. "Whatever may be the origin or cause of the 'rappings,' the ladies in whose presence they occur do not make them," Greeley told his readers. "We tested this thoroughly and to our entire satisfaction."

Inspired by the Fox sisters, other mediums started to come forward, and soon a new religious movement called Spiritualism was born. Spiritualists believed in God and in the power of ghosts to communicate with the living through mediums. They were inspired by the writing of Emanuel Swedenborg, a Swedish scientist and philosopher, who believed

Haunted Links

Want to find out more about the Fox sisters and other freaky paranormal stories? Check out the Discovery Channel's online Psychic and Paranormal Web site content. To find it, type "Discovery Channel Paranormal" into your search engine.

that people could make contact with a vast spirit world by carefully tuning their senses.

Because of public séances by people like the Fox sisters, Spiritualism quickly became very popular in the United States and Britain, and it had many famous supporters, including Sir Arthur Conan Doyle, the writer who created the legendary detective Sherlock Holmes. While Spiritualism is not as popular as it was a hundred years ago, there are still Spiritualist churches throughout the world.

In the end, the story of the Fox sisters and the religious movement they helped found does not provide a final answer to our question: Do ghosts really exist? Late in her life, Maggie said that it had all been a hoax. She explained that she had produced the mysterious rappings by cracking the joint in her big toe. While this explanation satisfied the skeptics, it didn't convince the thousands of people who had seen the Fox sisters in action. How did they make objects fly around the room? How could those in attendance mistake the sound of a toe cracking for loud knocking that seemed to resonate all around the room? Maggie couldn't – or wouldn't – answer these questions.

The mystery continues to this day.

THE FAMOUS GHOSTS

While some ghosts prefer to hide in walls and rap on tables, others seem to enjoy a more public life. Many people who were famous in life, remain famous in death. Here's a quick look at just some of the historical figures whose ghosts are said to have returned to haunt the living.

Nero. Famous for fiddling while Rome burned, Roman Emperor Nero committed suicide in 68 CE. Years later, the locals believed that his ghost was trapped inside his tomb, and that a flock of ravens congregated in a nearby walnut tree each day to torment the restless spirit. The ghost grew noisier and unhappier until the locals could not stand it anymore. Around 1110 CE, they asked the Pope to get rid of the spirit. He performed a special ceremony called an exorcism, designed to get rid of evil spirits. It worked. Nero's ghost hasn't been heard from since.

Dante Alighieri. One of the most famous poets ever, Dante wrote *The Divine Comedy*, which tells the story of a man's trip through hell, guided by a ghost. In real life, part of Dante's poem went missing after he died. The family almost gave up trying to find the lost pages – until one night when Dante's ghost visited his son Jacobo in a dream. The ghost led him to one of the other rooms in the family home and pointed to a hidden compartment. As soon as he woke up, Jacobo raced to the spot and found the final missing verses of the poem.

Anne Boleyn. Anne was the second wife of England's notorious King Henry the VIII. After the Pope refused to let the couple divorce, King Henry had Anne beheaded. Anne's ghost has probably been seen more times than any other spirit. More than thirty thousand sightings have been reported since her death in 1536. She is most often seen in the Tower of London – one of the most haunted places in the world – and frequently appears carrying her head in her hands.

Marie Antoinette. This famous queen also lost her head over politics. She was executed by guillotine during the French Revolution in 1793, and visitors to the royal palace at Versailles now regularly see Marie's ghost wandering the halls, wearing a pink dress and hat from the period.

Napoleon Bonaparte. Napoleon was a great military leader who became Emperor of France following the Revolution. After his armies were defeated, he was exiled to Elba, a tiny island off Italy in the Atlantic. News traveled slowly back then – there were no TVs, cell phones, or even telegraphs. But on the day Napoleon died, May 5, 1821, a mysterious man visited his mother in Rome. He told her that her son had died then quietly disappeared before she could ask him any questions. How could the stranger know about something that had just happened on a remote island more than six hundred miles away? Many believe it was the ghost of Napoleon himself, who'd returned to his mother one last time to deliver the sad news.

Ivan the Terrible. Ivan's ghost is reported to haunt Moscow's Kremlin, headquarters of the country's government. The ghost is said to be just as terrifying as Ivan was in real life when he was ruthless ruler of Russia in the sixteenth century, with a flaming face and an angry disposition. His appearance is considered to be a bad omen, as he often appears right before the death of a leader or some other political upheaval.

Abraham Lincoln. America's most famous president is also one of the country's most famous ghosts. Said to haunt the White House, Lincoln's ghost was first spotted in the 1920s by Grace Coolidge, wife of President Calvin Coolidge. Years later, Ronald Reagan said that the ghost of Lincoln could still be felt in the White House. In fact, one of his dogs barked every time he passed Lincoln's old bedroom, and the dog refused to ever go in the room. It's no surprise that Lincoln's spirit is still with us. Not only did he die tragically, but during his lifetime, Lincoln is known to have had paranormal experiences. He once told friends about a dream he had where he saw a man lying in a casket. He asked a guard to tell him who had died. The guard replied, "President Lincoln." Three days later, Lincoln was shot and killed.

THE NASTY GHOSTS

Some are famous, others are notorious. Poltergeists are some of the freakiest ghosts around.

Known for rattling furniture, throwing objects around rooms, and even pushing and biting people, these special ghosts have a long and distinguished history.

The word *poltergeist* comes from the German for "noisy ghost," which makes sense since the first recorded poltergeist haunting took place in that country. It dates back almost twelve hundred years, when an unseen spirit tormented a family for months. The spirit shook the walls, threw stones, and generally made life miserable for the poor people. Finally, a contingent of priests arrived to try and rid the house of the spirit – only to be sent packing by the ghost, which pelted them with stones.

Our history books tell us of many other celebrated poltergeist

Is Seeing Believing?

Does a videotape from a security camera provide proof that ghosts exist?

The setting is London's Hampton Court, a palace built by King Henry VIII, one of the most haunted places in that city of haunts. Here's the story. Late one night, just before Christmas 2003, security guards in the palace responded to alarm bells going off. The bells suggested that one of the doors was opening – and that could mean that someone was trying to break into the historic castle. The guards quickly checked all the doors and walked around the grounds. There was nothing. No doors open, no signs of intruders.

Curious, they reviewed all the security camera tapes. What they found was electrifying. A tape from one camera, mounted outside and facing the main court-yard, showed an eerie figure dressed in old-fashioned clothes. The set of doors leading to the courtyard opened by itself, then the ghostly figure emerged and angrily slammed the doors shut.

Is the video for real? So far, there is no evidence of a hoax – and the palace was secured and under surveillance when the apparition appeared. It looks authentic, but why take our word for it? Type "Hampton Court Ghost Video" into your favorite search engine and judge for yourself.

hauntings. These are just a few. Experiences with these testy spirits are not uncommon.

The Drummer of Tedworth. This story from the 1600s takes place in a small town in England, where an argument between neighbors set off a strange set of circumstances. A wealthy landowner named John Mompesson sued his neighbor, a drummer, and was awarded his drum in payment. Soon afterward, Mompesson's children were awoken to the sound of an unseen hand drumming on the headboards of their beds. It wasn't long before objects began moving around the kitchen and an invisible hand started throwing shoes and stones at Mompesson and his family. Mompesson accused the drummer of using witchcraft to create the disturbances . . . and, in turn, gave paranormal researchers one of the first recorded examples of a poltergeist haunting.

The Ghost of Derrygonnelly. This Irish poltergeist invaded a farmer's home in the 1870s. The spirit made noises at all hours of the night and moved objects around as the farmer and his children watched. This was investigated by a local doctor named William Barrett, who at first believed it was all a trick. But he changed his mind after the poltergeist repeatedly passed a simple test. Barrett would think of a number and then ask the spirit to knock out that number. This was one of the first attempts to study a poltergeist. The Ghost of Derrygonnelly continued to be studied by researchers for almost a century.

The Bell Witch. Perhaps the most famous poltergeist in American history, the story of the Bell Witch began when John Bell encountered a strange beast while out hunting near his home in rural Tennessee. The animal had the body of a dog and the head of a rabbit. Soon afterward,

The Bell Witch House

strange things started happening in the Bell home. It began with scratching and growling noises around the outside of the house. Soon, the children's blankets and pillows were pulled off them as they lay in bed. In time, odd voices could be heard as the poltergeist seemed to focus its attention on Bell's youngest daughter, Betsy. The unruly spirit would pull her hair and slap her with such force that it left marks on her arms and face. The ghostly visitations stopped as suddenly as they started, and no one has ever been able to explain exactly what caused these strange attacks.

2. SCIENCE VERSUS FICTION
Scientists and Paranormal Researchers Take a Closer Look at Ghosts

IT'S ONE OF THE MOST curious ghost stories ever.

It concerns a certain man named Phillip Aylesford, a seventeenth-century British aristocrat, married to the daughter of a powerful nobleman. Phillip lived a life of luxury, but he wasn't happy. Although he and his wife had everything they could wish for, they no longer loved one another.

One day, Phillip was out riding his horse when he came across a gypsy camp. In the midst of it, he saw a beautiful, dark-haired gypsy girl. He took her back to his estate and gave her a job as a servant. Soon, they fell in love.

Eventually, Phillip's wife found out about the gypsy girl. She accused the girl of witchcraft, had her tried in court. Eventually she was burned at the stake.

Phillip stood by in silence through the whole ordeal. He was afraid that if he spoke up and defended the gypsy girl, he would lose his reputation and good standing in the community. Over time, though, the loss of the girl's love and the memory of his cowardice made Phillip very sad. One night, he could stand it no more: he jumped from a high tower and plunged to his death.

Three hundred years later, at a special séance in Canada, the ghost of Phillip returned. It was 1972, and – channeled by members of the Toronto Society for Psychical Research – Phillip moved objects, lifted a table off the ground, and communicated through a series of coded raps. And best of all, the entire séance was caught on film.

Is this proof positive that ghosts exist?

Well, not exactly.

Spirit Links

Want to see Phillip Aylesford in action? Type "phillip.mov reality twist" into a video search engine to find an amazing documentary. It tells the story of this fascinating experiment, and it shows actual footage of the table moving and rising as well as Phillip's other attempts to communicate with the here and now.

You see, the most remarkable thing about Phillip was that he was entirely made up.

It was all in the name of science. A group of members from the Toronto Society for Psychical Research had a theory – that the human mind has powerful abilities we barely understand. They believed that ghosts and other paranormal phenomena were actually the result of brain waves in action, and they called this process psychokinesis.

One member came up with the story of an imaginary ghost she called Phillip. Then eight members of the research team put on a series of séances and tried to conjure up Phillip's spirit. For weeks, nothing happened. They sat around a small table, a drawing of Phillip in the center, and concentrated.

Eventually, though, some of the members started to feel the table vibrate. Over the following weeks, the vibrations became more obvious until finally the table was moving slowly across the floor.

In time, "Phillip" communicated through a series of coded raps, and objects moved around the room by themselves. Even the table slid and rose dramatically.

Was this the work of psychokinetic energy, as the researchers believed? Or was it just some passing spirit that decided to take advantage of a séance and a captive audience to make contact with the living? No one knows for sure. But what we do know is that there are a lot of strange things going on, and researchers are continuing to try and separate science from fiction.

GHOSTS UNDER THE MICROSCOPE

With the success of the Fox sisters and the rise of Spiritualism, the modern era of Ghost Tracking began. People became more and more fascinated with ghosts and the paranormal and wanted to find out if these otherworldly phenomena were for real.

The Society for Psychical Research was one of the first organizations to take up the call. Founded in London, England, in 1882, the society aimed to take a scientific approach to the investigation of paranormal activity ("psychical" is a fancy word for the term "psychic forces"). It was a very prestigious organization. Well-known scientists, professors, writers – even a future prime minister – joined the society and supported its research.

The members quickly got to work, and within a few years, they produced *Phantasms of the Living*, a study of over seven hundred reports of ghost sightings. It was a huge step forward, the first time anyone had taken a serious scientific approach to studying the paranormal. The book was soon followed by other major studies that took a close look at things like ghostly visitations, telepathy, and spirit mediums. And along the way, the society exposed a number of frauds and hoaxes.

The Society for Psychical Research continues its work to this day. The British organization has been joined by similar research groups in countries like Canada and the United States, along with dozens of ghost-hunting clubs around the world. The efforts of these early paranormal researchers have helped paved the way for today's Ghost Trackers.

PRICE IS RIGHT

If there's one person who did more than anyone else to popularize ghost hunting, it's Harry Price.

Born in England in 1881 in the middle of the spirit and medium frenzy that was sweeping the English-speaking world, Price grew up to become the most famous and widely read paranormal researcher of the era.

Price first caught the public's attention through his work exposing paranormal

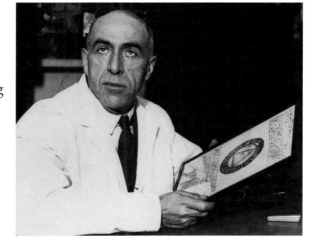

Harry Price

fakes. As more and more people got caught up in the Spiritualism craze, con artists and thieves began to see the paranormal as their chance to trick people out of their money. A number of marginal mediums toured the séance circuit, using magic tricks, sleight of hand, and other deceptions to convince people that they were for real.

One of these scam artists was a man named William Hart, who'd made a name as a spirit photographer. It was a simple deception. Hart would take a picture of a person. When he developed the photo, he would superimpose the image of another person dressed as a ghost onto the original image. If you looked at one of these pictures today, you would know right away that it was a phony. But this was back when photography was a new and mysterious process; most people did not know that you could easily superimpose one image onto another.

Price investigated the spirit photographer's work and announced to the world that Hart was a fake.

The publicity made Price famous, and he soon set up his own Laboratory for Psychical Research, using money he had inherited to help finance the lab's investigative work. Over time, Price investigated thousands of spirit mediums, haunted houses, and ghost sightings, concluding that only one in a thousand reports of paranormal activity proved to be real.

Price went to great lengths to investigate these cases, and he used technology that was even more sophisticated than anything used by the best con artists of the time. Once, Price attended a séance by Rudi Schneider, an Austrian medium that even Price believed was the real deal. Just to be sure though, Price rigged up a special device that could measure small changes in pressure being applied to the séance table's surface. The device triggered an infrared camera, which uses a special kind of light that's invisible to the human eye, to take pictures in the dark. (Today's night-vision video cameras use the same light.)

During the séance, Schneider secretly reached behind his back to grab a handkerchief and throw it onto the floor. The change in pressure on the table from Schneider lifting his arm triggered the infrared camera. Everybody at the séance thought it was a spirit moving the cloth, but Price's trap caught the truth on film.

Still, it wasn't the fakes that interested Price as much as the stories that seemed to be authentic. He investigated many sites, including the Tower of London and Borley Rectory, the most haunted buildings in all of England. He was most impressed, though, by the work of two psychics. One was a French clairvoyant named Jeanne Laplace. When Price first

Can Houdini Escape Death?

Harry Houdini is remembered as the greatest escape artist and magician of all time. But does he have one more trick up his sleeve?

Before his death – on Halloween in 1926 – Houdini promised his wife, Bess, that if there was any way to break free from the afterlife and get a message to her, he would find it.

It was an interesting promise from a man who, back then, was just as famous for exposing paranormal fakes as he was for his daring escapes.

Remember, it was still the golden age of Spiritualism, and organizations like the Society for Psychical Research and Harry Price's famous laboratory were determined to expose hoaxes and find proof of the paranormal.

Houdini had become interested in Spiritualism when his mother died. But his attempts to contact her through spirit mediums all failed, and he came to believe that most of them were just scam

artists. Of course, being a professional magician, it was easy for him to figure out if a medium was using tricks!

Disillusioned with Spiritualism, Houdini traveled the world, exposing fake mediums wherever he found them. Still, his experiences did not dampen his belief in life after death, and he was convinced that some spirits were real. And so he made his pact with Bess.

The result?

Every year since Houdini's death more than nine decades ago, family and fans have held a special séance on Halloween night at the site of the magician's grave, in Machpelah Cemetery in Brooklyn, New York. Armed with secret code (which Houdini passed on to his wife when he died), the Houdini faithful have been waiting patiently for his spirit to break through and make contact. He hasn't escaped death yet. But if anyone can do it, it's Harry Houdini.

met with her, he silently gave her a photograph of a young girl. Laplace then went on to make thirty-four very detailed and clear statements about the girl, which all proved to be true. She even got the girl's name right – Mary – even though Price thought the girl's name was actually Mollie. It was only later, when Price checked the girl's birth certificate, that he discovered Madam Laplace was right and he was wrong!

Of all the cases he investigated, Price thought the most amazing one concerned the ghost of an air force pilot known as Lieutenant Irwin. Within forty-eight hours of dying in a plane crash, the ghost visited a Mrs. Eileen Garrett, a British medium, giving her a highly detailed description of the plane crash. As Price told *Time* magazine for a 1936 article, Eileen did "not know one end of an airship from another." Still, the ghost of Lieutenant Irwin "gave particulars of the R-101 which were semi-official secrets, and which afterwards were confirmed at the public inquiry." Price was convinced that the ghost of Irwin, and Garrett's psychic powers, were for real.

Harry conducted investigations for more than thirty years, along the way writing dozens of books and scientific articles, exposing hundreds of frauds, and studying hundreds of mysteries that remain unsolved to this day. His laboratory became the center of paranormal research, and he even helped set up the Council for Psychical Research at the University of London.

Was he the world's first Ghost Tracker? Maybe not, but he sure helped popularize a scientific approach to investigating paranormal activity and he laid the groundwork for generations of ghost hunters to come.

THE QUEST CONTINUES

Scientists and researchers are still searching for definitive proof to determine whether ghosts are figments or for real. Despite almost a century of serious study, no one seems closer to the truth.

Part of the problem is that ghosts and other paranormal phenomena are difficult for scientists to study. Science, after all, is about observation and measurement. If you can't see something, weigh it, find out how long it is, it's pretty hard to examine. Also, when something is as unpredictable as a ghost, it's near impossible to know when to look.

To complicate matters, people disagree on what a ghost actually is. There are lots of theories. Some people, for example, believe ghosts are the product of some unknown energy force. Not long ago, people did not know about electricity, magnetism, or radio waves. When they saw lightning, they believed it was the work of some supernatural being – a god or spirit – and not the result of natural forces at work.

Other people speculate that ghosts are shadows from another dimension, going about their daily business unaware that they are causing a stir. Again, this theory could be true. Scientists now hypothesize that there are dozens of dimensions to go along with the ones we are most familiar with, like time and space. Who knows what wonders exist in these unexplored worlds?

Another theory maintains that ghosts are just in our heads. But the amazing part, according to this theory, is that somehow we are able to project thoughts from one mind to another. Ghosts, then, are part of a

How Did a TV Show Change the Way We Think About Ghosts?

In 1972, just around Christmastime, England's BBC aired a television special about a haunted house. Called *The Stone Tape*, the show was a made-up story about a group of scientists conducting a paranormal investigation.

In the special, one of the scientists came up with a theory. He believed that buildings and the materials used to make them were able to capture the energy from living beings. This energy could be imprinted on the building, recording an image of a person that could be played back over time, almost like a video camera. Of course, old buildings were often made of stone, not videotape, so these phantom recordings are made on "stone tape."

The scientist in the show believed that this psychic energy is at its strongest (and therefore more likely to be recorded) when people are under emotional stress. That's why stories of murders, suicides, and torture are often associated with haunted houses.

The show was popular when it was broadcast, and the central idea has caught on with paranormal researchers. Today, the Stone Tape Theory is widely accepted by ghost hunters, who believe it helps account for phenomena like residual ghosts and even some poltergeist activities. It's an ongoing tribute to a TV show that changed the way we think about ghosts and haunted houses.

telepathic connection between two or more minds, kind of like a video our brain downloads from some unknown place and replays in a way that makes it seem real. Psychokinesis and our friendly phantom Phillip are a good example of this brain-wave theory.

Then of course there's the good old-fashioned theory that argues that ghosts are spirits of dead people who have come back to the world of the living. Maybe they have some unfinished business to complete. Maybe they are stuck in a strange place, somewhere between this world and the next. Maybe they are just plain lonely and crave the company of living beings.

Are any of these theories true? Could they all have a part to play? Or are ghosts really just made up, the result of tricks and hoaxes and our imaginations running wild?

So far, most paranormal research has focused on things that can be controlled in an experiment. Rather than sitting in a haunted house hoping that a ghost shows up, scientists have been exploring things like ESP, mind-over-matter, and telepathy. The results have been interesting. One of the most famous studies, conducted by a scientist named Joseph Rhine in the 1930s, found that some people actually seem to possess ESP, the ability to read other people's minds. In his test, Rhine had one person look at a special card. Then another person, without looking, would try and guess what card it was. Time and time again, people who felt that they had psychic abilities were often able to guess the correct cards, suggesting that maybe there are some unknown forces at work.

More recently, scientists have discovered something even more amazing. Scientists studying the way macaque monkeys think and communicate came across a small cluster of cells in the monkey's brain that has a very special function. Called mirror neurons, these cells allow monkeys to imitate each other's actions, understand others' emotions, and even read their minds.

We now know that humans and other primates have these mirror neurons too, and they help us understand the thoughts and feelings of others. They kick into action whenever we see or imitate someone else's behavior, or even when we watch someone do something that interests us in some way. The mirror cells in our brain behave exactly the same way as cells in the brain of the person we are watching.

While this discovery might one day help us better understand how children learn complex tasks, like talking, some researchers believe that it might also provide the key to understanding such paranormal phenomena as ESP and telepathy.

The research continues, and Ghost Trackers like you keep up their investigations, hoping to solve the mystery and become the first to find proof that ghosts are either fact or fiction.

3. WHO'S THAT GHOUL?
A Guide to Spirits, Ghosts, and Other Apparitions

IT'S ONE OF THE MOST FAMOUS ghost photographs of all time: a vaporous, ghostly shape descending a stairway in an old English mansion.

They call the ghost the Brown Lady of Raynham Hall (brown for the color of the dress worn by the misty form), which has reportedly wandered historic Raynham Hall in Norfolk, England, for centuries.

The Brown Lady

The ghost, of course, is a story in its own right. The Brown Lady is believed to be the spirit of Lady Mary Townsend (wife of a hot-tempered nobleman), who died a virtual prisoner in her home over three hundred years ago. According to the legend, after husband Charles Townsend convinced himself that his wife was in love with another man, he locked her inside their huge country estate. He refused to allow her any visitors, and he even prevented their children from seeing her.

Not long after her death, strange reports of a ghostly figure began to emerge from the hall. The stories were always similar. An old woman appeared, dressed in brown, and there was a look of extreme sadness on her ashen face. Dozens of people saw the figure, even George IV, King of England, who stayed the night in Raynham Hall in the early 1800s.

Ghosts weren't exactly on the minds of photographers Captain Robert Provand and Indre Shira when they visited the hall in 1936. At that point, sightings of the Brown Lady had become very rare, and the two men were on assignment for *Country Life* magazine to do a photo essay on the quaint, old home. They were looking for pretty pictures, not ghosts.

One afternoon, as they were taking pictures of the curious furnishings and dramatic architecture, the photographers had an unexpected encounter. According to Shira's report for *Country Life*, Provand had just taken one photograph of the majestic main staircase and was preparing to take another. This took a little work because cameras then were big and bulky, and the photographer had to cover his head and part of the camera with a black cloth to prevent light from leaking in and ruining the shot.

As Provand got set, Shira stood by his side, looking directly up the staircase.

"All at once," Shira told his readers, "I detected an ethereal veiled form coming slowly down the stairs. Rather excitedly, I called out sharply: 'Quick, quick, there's something.' I pressed the trigger of the flashlight pistol. After the flash and on closing the shutter, Captain Provand removed the focusing cloth from his head and turning to me said: 'What's all the excitement about?'"

The "excitement" turned out to be the Brown Lady herself, slowly making her way down the stairs. And Provand had captured her on film.

The picture went on to be an international sensation, and it is still considered one of the best spirit photographs ever taken.

For today's Ghost Trackers it's especially interesting. Not only does it suggest that Raynham Hall would be the perfect place for an investigation, but it also forces the question: What exactly are we looking at? The picture shows a fuzzy, glowing object – more of a radiant object than a human form. It appears to be what paranormal researchers call a ghost light or ectoplasm.

The thing is, when we talk about ghosts, we are actually talking about a range of phenomena. Everything from strange lights to walking, talking spirits to poltergeists that can move objects and even bite or scratch (although they are rarely seen) – all these fall under the label "ghost."

In this chapter, then, we're going to take a closer look at the different types of ghosts, to better understand the kinds of things a good Ghost Tracker is looking for. Of course, there are no hard and fast rules when it comes to classifying ghosts and spirits, but these are some of the popular apparitions that wind up on every Ghost Tracker's must-see list.

ORBS, PLASMOIDS, STREAMERS, AND VORTICES

The most common kind of apparition, orbs can be found almost anywhere strange phenomena have been encountered. They appear as small, round lights that often move quickly in an erratic pattern.

The best way to see orbs is not with the naked eye, but with a camera. You've probably already seen pictures of orbs. They are those unexplainable little lights that show up on family photos, often on dark nights or in creepy, old buildings. Exactly what causes these orbs is open to debate. Some researchers think they are the souls of dead people. Others believe they are psychic or other unknown energy fields.

A word of caution, though. Not every strange ball of light you capture in a photograph will necessarily be an orb. Often, the light from your camera flash can reflect off raindrops, dust particles, and even flying insects to create an orb-like image in a photo. So how can you tell a real orb from a speck of dust floating in front of the camera?

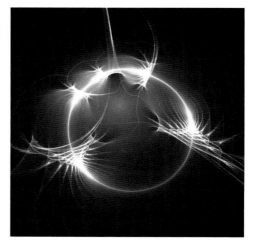

First of all, make sure your camera lens is clean, and avoid taking pictures in a dusty room or on a rainy night. Second, take a good, close look at the photograph. A photo with lots of orbs in it probably means that you have taken a nice picture of glowing dust. However, if you see a single round light that's fairly large in size and slightly fuzzy, you might have captured a photograph of a genuine orb.

Video cameras are also a great way to collect evidence of orbs. While it tends to be more difficult to get them on video, once you do, it's easier to convince skeptics that your moving orb is not just dust. One night, while filming the show *Ghost Trackers* in a historic theater that was once the scene of a mysterious murder, one of our Trackers videotaped himself looking into a large mirror. A while later, a second Ghost Tracker came down the grand staircase and videotaped himself in front of the same mirror. Only later, when we reviewed the tapes, did we realize that each video showed a moving orb, clearly visible in the mirror, near each Tracker. One orb could have been written off as some trick of the light – but a second orb in the same mirror? Something curious was definitely going on.

Plasmoids and streamers (or small, moving lights) are similar to orbs. The difference is that both these phenomena are much faster moving. Streamers appear to be trailing a tail of light or energy, like a tiny comet. Because they move so quickly, though – often appearing as a quick flash in your periphery vision – plasmoids and streamers are harder to see with the naked eye than orbs. Still, researchers often see them in photos taken during investigations of haunted locations.

A vortex is one of the most prized of all paranormal apparitions. Likely related to orbs, plasmoids, and streamers, vortices are funnel-shaped energy masses with a distinctive tread-mark shape in the center. They seem to come in limited colors – white or light blue – and most often go unnoticed until they show up in photographs or on video. Ghost Trackers are always on the lookout for an opportunity to study these phenomena further.

ECTOPLASM, GHOST LIGHTS, AND SHADOW GHOSTS

In the heyday of Spiritualism, almost a century ago, ectoplasm seemed to appear everywhere – either in the form of slimy, sticky goo or as fuzzy, swirling mist. It was thought that ectoplasm was the stuff of ghosts, and no medium worthy of the name would dare host a public séance without producing some of the sticky stuff, and early spirit photographs were full of these misty, half-formed phantoms.

Today, we know that much of the early ectoplasm craze was simple fakery at its worst. Samples of ectoplasm left behind at séances turned out to be nothing more than sticky strips of cloths or egg whites whipped with sugar. Tasty, perhaps, but hardly supernatural.

Photographs of ectoplasm taken today often prove to be fairly obvious forgeries too, created by superimposing one picture on top of another.

Still, the mystery of ectoplasm continues. While reports of sticky residue – like the ghostly goo that slimed Bill Murray in the movie *Ghost Busters* – are very rare these days, the appearance of a large mass of glowing, swirling mist is one of the most commonly reported paranormal sights.

The ectoplasm craze gave rise to fake photos.

Ectoplasm may have a vaguely human form, or it may be fairly shapeless. It appears and disappears quite suddenly. Ghost Trackers who have witnessed ectoplasm also report feeling a strong energy presence, a kind of electric tingling sensation.

Related to ectoplasm is the paranormal phenomenon known as ghost lights. Just like the name suggests, these are otherworldly lights with no obvious point of origin. Usually they are white or yellow, but they can come in any color, and they may change color during a single appearance. Ghostly lights are a big favorite of Ghost Trackers since they tend to be fairly reliable, often appearing over and over again in the same location.

Ghost lights have a long and distinguished history and are almost as well documented as ghosts themselves. One of the earliest reports of these strange lights dates back to 1656, when a small town in Wales was over-run with the luminous loomings. They appeared in houses, farmers' fields, churches – almost everywhere. A legend arose that the lights were a signal that someone in the village had died: a child's death was followed by the appearance of a small light, while the death of an adult would be signaled with a large light.

Some ghost lights are so dependable that they become tourist attractions of sorts. Just outside of Marfa, a small town in Texas, an official viewing platform has been set up so people can safely park at the side of the road and watch out for ghost lights. Originally reported in the 1880s by a farmer, the Marfa lights continue to this day, skipping across the night sky, delighting Ghost Trackers and mystifying scientists. Thousands of people have seen the Marfa lights, and they've taken photos and videotapes. The mystery remains.

Even more remarkable are the Brown Mountain ghost lights of North Carolina. For over a century, people have reported seeing strange, elongated lights drifting up and across the mountainside. According to legend, the lights began after a local woman disappeared. Many people suspected that her husband had killed her and left her body on the mountain. An extensive search revealed nothing, and the husband was never arrested.

Over time, the lights disappeared. But years later, someone came across the skeleton of a young woman in the mountain's underbrush. The mysterious lights returned again – and have been haunting the North Carolina night sky ever since.

Other prized catches for Ghost Trackers are shadow ghosts, also called shadow people. Almost the mirror opposite of ghost lights or ectoplasm, shadow ghosts are thin shadows that hide among the other shadows of the night. Ghost Trackers usually just catch a glimpse of a shadow ghost before it disappears. While they appear frequently during investigations, shadow ghosts are very difficult to photograph or videotape.

These apparitions tend to be completely black in color, and they usually lack any human features. In some cases, they are simply a formless mass, like a black ectoplasm.

Are Ghost Lights For Real?

When it comes to North Carolina's Brown Mountain ghost lights, the answer seems to be a resounding *yes*. The lights appear regularly, and they have been seen by thousands of people. And yet, after more than a hundred years of study, scientists still have no explanation. The U.S. highway department leaves no doubt that the lights exist. A highway department sign posted at a roadside stop, where people can pull over to look for the ghost lights, offers this simple summary.

The long, even-crested mountain in the distance is Brown Mountain. From early times, people have observed weird, wavering lights rise above this mountain, then dwindle and fade away.

CRISIS APPARITION

A crisis apparition is one of the most commonly reported kinds of paranormal phenomenon. Throughout history, people from all walks of life describe odd visits from friends, relatives, and even strangers that either signal the death of someone or help avert a tragedy.

Stories about crisis apparitions abound. One of my favorites concerns a miner. He was digging deep in a coal mine when he saw someone walking his way. It was a figure dressed in full mining gear, and it had a blank look on its face. The figure didn't speak or otherwise acknowledge the worker, it just kind of floated past him. The worker called out and followed the curious stranger, but as they went down a side tunnel, the mysterious miner slowly faded.

The miner shook his head and rubbed his eyes. Were they playing a trick on him?

What happened next was just as remarkable. The shaft where the miner had been working moments before suddenly collapsed. If he hadn't followed the phantom stranger, the worker would have been crushed under tons of rock.

Though the location and year of this story are now uncertain, the phantom miner is a perfect example of a crisis apparition. As in most cases of crisis apparitions, the spirit takes a human form but interacts very little with the humans it encounters. Also, the phantom minor appeared only once, for a brief time, then disappeared. Most crisis apparitions rarely appear

Crisis apparition or trick photography? This might be an example of a "Last Good-bye Spirit."

Did a Crisis Apparition Help Convict a Killer?

It was a crisis apparition with a conscience.

When the ghost of Zona Shue repeatedly visited her mother, it was to bring comfort or to warn of danger. And it was to try and help her mother solve the mystery of who had killed her daughter.

On January 23, 1897, a neighbor boy found Zona dead in her West Virginia farmhouse. She was lying at the bottom of the stairs, her head turned on a curious angle.

By the time the doctor arrived to examine her, Zona's husband, Erasmus, had already carried her upstairs to the bedroom. He had dressed her for burial, in one of her finest dresses that had a fashionably high collar.

Erasmus was understandably upset, and he refused to let go of his wife's body to allow the doctor to conduct a proper examination. The woman had probably fainted and fallen down the stairs, the doctor finally concluded. It was the best guess he could come up with under the circumstances.

Zona's mother, Mary Jane Heaster, had a different theory. She had never liked Erasmus, and now she suspected that he had had a hand in Zona's untimely death. But there was no police service to carry out a real investigation, and Mary Jane believed she would never find the truth.

But Zona had other ideas. Three weeks after the funeral, Zona's spirit visited Mary Jane in the middle of the night. It first appeared as a bright light that slowly formed into the shape of a woman, and then it told Mary Jane her grizzly tale. She'd been murdered by her husband, her neck broken in a vicious rage. To emphasize the point, the apparition rotated its head all the way around.

Zona's ghost visited her mother four nights in a row, telling the same story and rotating its head each time.

Finally, Mary Jane went to talk to the district attorney. She convinced the law officer to take another look at her daughter's case. The D.A. agreed and ordered an autopsy.

Zona's body was dug up and examined by a doctor. The findings were clear. Zona had died of a broken neck, the finger-shaped bruises still evident on her throat. Erasmus was charged with the crime and found guilty after a long trial. He was sentenced to life in prison – and he entered the history books as the first murderer ever convicted with the help of his victim's ghost.

more than once. Finally, even though the phantom miner clearly came for a reason (to warn the worker), like most crisis apparitions, it gave no direct indication of its purpose.

There appear to be three distinct kinds of crisis apparitions.

The most common is what I call the Last Good-bye Spirit, a ghost that comes to pay a final visit to a loved one, like Napoleon's good-bye appearance at his mother's house.

Helpful Spirits are otherworldly visitors like the phantom miner, which show up in the nick of time to save someone's life. These spirits often take the form of a silent, eerie being that is not known by the person who sees it.

Finally, there are the Messenger Spirits, ghosts that appear before one person in order to help or get information to another person.

The famous nineteenth century spirit that appeared to a prominent Philadelphia doctor named S. Weir Mitchell is an example of a Messenger Spirit. It was late one night when the doctor heard a knock on his door.

Mitchell found a girl waiting outside, dressed in rags, who asked the doctor to come quickly: her mother was sick and perhaps even on her deathbed.

The doctor followed the little girl through the snowy streets until they came to a small apartment. Inside, the doctor found a very sick, feverish woman. He quickly diagnosed the problem: she was suffering from pneumonia. He immediately administered medication, and soon the fever broke.

A few days later, the doctor went back to visit the woman. She was well on her way to recovery, and the doctor commented that she was very lucky that her daughter had come when she did; any further delay and the woman very likely could have died.

"My daughter . . . ," the woman said, in disbelief. "Doctor, my daughter died a month ago."

While crisis apparitions are common, they are very unpredictable. This makes them quite hard to investigate or study. Many Ghost Trackers go their whole lives without ever encountering one of these types of spirits face-to-face.

RESIDUAL GHOST

Probably the most frequent of all apparitions, residual ghosts seem to be tied to specific places, to replaying the same actions over and over again.

The sound of children playing, a ghostly figure that wanders a house checking each room as it goes, a spirit that watches from a high window – these kinds of reports of residual ghosts are common.

Many researchers believe that seeing a residual ghost is really like watching a movie play out in real life. The theory is that traumatic events – like a murder, suicide, or accidental death – trigger strong emotional responses and can create a lot of energy. This energy leaves an imprint on the location where the event happened. What you see, then, is less likely to be the spirit of a dead person; it's more a visible memory of them.

No one has been able to prove this theory. But it's interesting that most residual ghosts do appear at the site of some tragic event. It's particularly common to find these apparitions at the scene of a bloody battle. For example, many visitors to historic Fort York in Toronto, Canada, have reported seeing soldiers dressed in period uniforms of the early 1800s, marching through the nearby fields. The fort is the site of several bloody battles from this time, as well as an accidental explosion that killed several dozen people, and it appears to have an entire platoon of residual spirits "living" in it.

The phantom soldiers never seem to notice the living, and they go through their routines – marching, standing guard, and sometimes fighting. More than one visitor has reported feeling a ghostly hand tug on their arm or push them down, as if a spirit was trying to move them out of the line of fire.

POLTERGEIST

Maybe you've heard the tale. It concerns a burial vault near the village of Oistin on the island of Barbados and the strange things that happened to the coffins that were placed in that vault.

The story starts in 1807, with the death of a woman named Tomasina Goddard. After her funeral, Goddard's body was placed in a coffin and sealed in a burial vault, a small brick tomb below ground.

Two years later, a two-year-old girl, Mary Ann Chase, caught a fever and died. She too was buried in the vault. In 1812, Mary Ann's teenaged sister, Dorcas, committed suicide and was placed in the tomb.

So far, a sad story, but nothing particularly strange.

Two weeks after Dorcas's death though, her father, Thomas, died suddenly. When it came time to place his coffin in the vault, family and friends were shocked by what they found. Inside the sealed tomb, the three coffins had all been moved around.

The family decided that someone was merely playing some kind of sick joke on them. But in 1816, the vault was opened for two more caskets. This time, all four coffins had been rearranged, including that of

Burial Vault

Thomas Chase, who'd been buried in a special lead-lined coffin weighing more than three hundred pounds. Whoever – or whatever – was moving these coffins had to be mighty powerful.

This time, once the old coffins were returned to their original places and the new coffins interred, the

Can a Poltergeist actually Hurt Someone?

While most poltergeists are fairly harmless, and some can even be quite playful, there are a few reported cases where things got ugly.

One of the most famous cases involves a Romanian girl named Eleonore Zugun. Her story begins in 1923, when objects suddenly started moving on their own in the eleven year old's home. At first, they were only small objects, like stones pelting the windows and knives and forks moving across the table on their own.

Soon, though, bigger objects started moving too. A water jug rose and floated through the air; a heavy trunk began to shake violently. And then things got personal.

Eleonore began experiencing the sensations of someone slapping her face, scratching her arm, and even biting her hands. The most frightening part was that these painful sensations left real marks on the poor girl. When she felt like she was being bitten, teeth marks would appear on her skin; when she felt like she had just been slapped, her cheek would turn red and hot.

Eleonore's story spread around the world, and famed Ghost Tracker Harry Price invited her to his Laboratory for Psychical Research in London, England. There, the phantom attacks continued in plain view of Price and the other researchers.

This isn't the only case of a person physically tormented by a poltergeist. In December 1965, strange things started happening in the Ferreira home in San Paulo, Brazil. Again, it started small, with stones and pieces of brick flying through the house, seemingly coming from nowhere. In time, larger objects started moving around and the poltergeist's activity became more violent. Pictures were torn from the walls, dishes were dashed on the floor, and tables and chairs were knocked over and tossed about.

The activity seemed to revolve around Maria José Ferreira, who, like Eleonore Zugun years before, was eleven when the disturbances started. And just as with Eleonore, Maria José's poltergeist attack soon turned personal. Maria José was slapped and bitten, and she frequently had pins stuck into her flesh by an unseen hand. Doctors once removed fifty tiny pins from her heel!

In both cases, the poltergeist attacks stopped as suddenly as they started. And despite the best efforts of researchers, no one has ever been able to explain what was really happening to the girls.

governor of the island ordered the vault sealed with cement. No one could get in – or out.

Yet, when the tomb was unsealed three years later to add more caskets, the coffins had been switched again.

Before closing the vault this time, the governor sprinkled sand on the floor, hoping to catch the culprit's footprints, and when the tomb was sealed, he left the imprint of his official stamp in the drying cement.

A year later, the tomb was opened. Again, the people of the town found the coffins had all been moved around, although there were no footprints in the sand and the governor's seal had not been broken.

That was it. The people of the island had had enough. The governor ordered workers to remove all the coffins and find another place to bury them. The vault was left open, and it has never been used again.

Today, the story of the Chase Vaults remains one of the most enduring paranormal mysteries of all time, and it is a perfect example of one of the strangest – and scariest – kinds of apparition: the poltergeist.

What exactly are poltergeists? Poltergeists are troublesome spirits that like to make their presence felt, often in haunted houses. Rarely seen, they will frequently move objects, make loud noises, touch people, and even produce strange smells that seem to come from nowhere. These can make for good investigations because they usually go on for an extended period of time.

Researchers have noticed that these spirits often seem to center around teenagers, especially teenage girls, or families with teenagers. (The Chase poltergeist, for example, first appeared after the death of Dorcas, a teenager at the time.) The belief is that these noisy ghosts are either some kind of energy that is attracted to adolescents or subconsciously created by them.

SPIRITS

Spirits have distinct personalities and seem to be free to do, more or less, as they please – unlike apparitions, which appear to have a fixed role or pattern. Spirits tend to interact with Ghost Trackers and others, and they leave evidence of their presence – everything from smells to temperature changes. Ghost Trackers often feel that they are being watched or touched by these spirits. Some researchers consider poltergeists to be a subset of spirits. We disagree. While most poltergeists never take on a physical appearance, spirits often do.

Faces of Belmez

The supernatural is hard to explain. While researchers are still trying to understand the nature of ghosts and apparitions, we at least have a number of working theories. But none of these can account for the Phantom Faces of Belmez.

The story began thirty-five years ago in a small Spanish town called Belmez de la Moraleda. Maria Gomez Pereira was doing odd jobs at the family home when she noticed strange stains around the fireplace in her kitchen. The stains formed a curious shape: together they looked eerily like the face of a woman.

Maria tried to wipe the stains away, but no matter how hard she scrubbed, the face remained.

Finally, frightened and frustrated, Maria had her husband dig up the floor tile with a pickax. They put in a new tile, but within weeks, new faces were forming.

Friends and neighbors started spreading the news of these strange phantom faces, and as new images appeared on the tile, the city council got involved. They ordered an investigation and had the floor dug up. Several feet down, workers made a shocking discovery: they found skeletons dating back almost six hundred years, and many of them were missing their skulls.

The bones were removed, and the kitchen floor was replaced. But within weeks, new images began to form. Many people began to think that the Pereira family was at the center of some elaborate hoax, so the city council stepped in again. This time, workers coated the tiles in a layer of wax and added some security measures to ensure that no one could tamper with the tiles. A number of weeks later, they removed the wax coating to find that new images had appeared.

Despite being investigated by numerous scientists and paranormal researchers, the mystery of the Phantom Faces of Belmez has never been solved. The faces continue to appear to this day, defying explanation, science, and common sense.

DO ANIMALS HAVE AN AFTERLIFE?

Humans aren't the only creatures to leave their ghostly impressions on the world. Reports of spirit animals have been common for centuries. Here are just a few of our favorite animal ghosts.

The Demonic Black Dog of Newgate Prison Sightings of ghostly black dogs are common around the world. These dogs are usually very scary, with red eyes that glow in the dark and menacing personalities. One of the most famous spirit dogs was said to haunt Newgate Prison, London's main jail. The demon dog first appeared four hundred years ago, after the starving prisoners killed and ate one of the inmates (who'd been accused of witchcraft). According to legend, the black dog took revenge on the cannibals, hunting each one of them down and killing them. The black spirit dog is still seen roaming the streets near where the jail once stood.

The Haunted Horses of Casa Loma Once home to an eccentric millionaire, the modern castle, built between 1911 and 1914, in Toronto, Canada, now boasts a number of haunted houseguests, including several horses. The wealthy Sir Henry Pellatt had an underground passageway built between the castle and the stables so he could keep a close eye on his favorite horses. To this day, people wandering through the passageway report hearing the sounds of hooves on the cobblestone floor and invisible horses whinnying in the distance.

Squire Cabell's Hounds Arthur Conan Doyle based his famous Sherlock Holmes novel *The Hound of Baskervilles* on the true story of Richard Cabell and the pack of haunting hounds that have been frequently spotted near his grave in Buckfastleigh, England. Rumor has it that Cabell murdered his wife in a jealous rage one mist-shrouded night. When her dog leaped at him to protect her, Cabell stabbed and killed the hound as well. Every year, on the anniversary of his death in 1677, Cabell's ghost is said to walk the moors with a pack of ghostly hounds, their fiery eyes glowing in the night.

Mesa Stampede Do cows have ghosts? Well, if you believe the story of the Mesa Stampede, the answer is *yes*. The story dates back to the late 1800s when a team of cowboys was leading one thousand five hundred longhorn cattle through the mountains of Texas. They decided to stop overnight in a grassy plateau, or mesa, to rest. It was a beautiful spot, with lush grassland bordered by a cliff with a sheer drop of one hundred feet to the valley below. Unfortunately, an old cowpoke who was driving his own small herd through the same area also wanted to rest in the mesa for the night. Angry that the bigger herd was taking his spot, the old cowboy caused a stampede, driving all but three hundred of the longhorns over the cliff to their death. The old man tried to escape, but the cowboys caught up with him and handed down their own form of justice. They blindfolded the old man, put him on his horse, and drove the pair over the cliff to meet the same fate as the cattle. To this day, visitors to the spot hear the sound of a phantom stampede, and many have claimed to see the ghost of an old cowboy, blindfolded and on horseback, going over the cliff to replay, in spirit world, his ghastly final moments on earth.

Know Your Stuff

Thanks to decades of research, Ghost Trackers have been able to identify several distinct types of ghostly phenomena. Do you know your ectoplasm from your plasmoids? Take this fun test, and match up the entity's name with its characteristics.

Name	Distinguishing Characteristics
1. Crisis Apparition	a. The most common kind of phenomenon at a haunting. It looks like a small ball of swirling light that either glows or is see-through.
2. Poltergeist	b. This is a light with no obvious point of origin. It usually appears as white or yellow, but it can come in any color, and it may change color during a single appearance.
3. Ectoplasm	c. These are similar to orbs, only fast moving and usually with a trailing tail of light or energy.
4. Plasmoid and Streamer	d. A ghost that appears only a few times to warn people about impending danger. This ghost usually takes human form.
5. Residual Ghost	e. A kind of haunting where the ghost or apparition does not seem to notice you. It's as if it is replaying a scene from its past life over and over again.
6. Ghost Light	f. A troublesome spirit that likes to make its presence felt. Rarely seen, it will often move objects, make loud noises, and touch people.
7. Orb	g. A very common kind of phenomenon, this appears as either a sticky, gooey substance or as a glowing, swirling mist. It may have a vaguely human form or be fairly shapeless.
8. Vortex	h. A prized catch for Ghost Trackers, this black spirit often hides among the other shadows of the night.
9. Shadow Ghost	i. Possibly related to an orb, this is a funnel-shaped energy mass with a distinctive swirl in the center.

Answers

1-d. 2-f. 3-g. 4-c. 5-e. 6-b. 7-a. 8-i. 9-h.

4. HAPPY HAUNTING GROUNDS
Exploring the World of Haunted Houses

A SMALL, TWO-STOREY HOUSE sits on the crest of a hill in a quiet wooded area just outside of Toronto, Canada. It's a simple structure, built almost two hundred years ago by Thomas Helliwell, a successful businessman who owned the nearby lumber mill and brewery.

Like many old houses, it has a colorful history. Over the years, many people lived, and died, in that house. Some died peacefully in their sleep, quietly passing away after a long, full life. But others died under much more tragic circumstances.

Helliwell House

Early in the house's history, Thomas's wife, Elizabeth, died while giving birth to a son. Two years later, that toddler fell into equipment at the nearby lumber mill. He was crushed to death. Not long after that, another one of Elizabeth's older children fell into the millstream and drowned.

Today, the house is part of a living museum, where visitors from around the world come to see how pioneers lived two centuries ago. Thousands of people visit the house each year, and while many of them probably think that the place would be the perfect setting for a horror movie about a haunted house, few people realize that they are passing through one of the eeriest places in the country.

A True Tale of Haunting?

An indistinct noise of what sounded like irregular tottering footsteps at length reached my ear. I listened with a beating heart and an undefined dread, fearing the sounds were the precursor of something terrible. Nor did my apprehension deceive me. A noise as violent struggling ensued, followed by a dreadful groan which seemed to roll upon my ear out of the pitchy darkness in which my room was shrouded. And such a groan, so long, deep and agonizing, surely never fell on mortal ears before.

– From "A Night in a Haunted House," a true ghost story from a magazine called the *Southern Literary Messenger*. The story was published anonymously in 1855. As a side note, famed horror writer Edgar Allan Poe was once editor of the *Messenger*.

Is Helliwell House haunted? Although there is no hard evidence, reports suggest that not only is it haunted, but it is also the site of intense paranormal activity. Most of the people who work at the museum have had a strange encounter or two. Their stories range from hearing strange sounds – a baby crying, children playing, footsteps on the stairs, and the soft voice of a woman speaking – to seeing shadows and encountering an actual ghost. The ghost appears as the figure of a woman, dressed in white, that lets off an otherworldly glow. She is silent and seems calm and welcoming, and she often appears to be searching for something.

It's a pretty cool story. So cool, in fact, that we decided to make Helliwell House the first place we ever investigated for the *Ghost Trackers* TV series.

I still remember the night we arrived to set up our remote-control cameras. It was a moonlit evening, and the house rose out of the darkness, half hidden by trees. A chill went up my spine. As I entered the house to help set things up, I was overcome by the creepiest feelings. It felt like being around someone who was very sad.

Weirder still, when I came out of the house, I noticed that my watch had stopped. This seemed odd because it had never stopped before. I gave it a shake, and it started again. I went into the house three more times that night, and each time I came out, I discovered my watch had stopped again.

That night, I witnessed one of the scariest paranormal events I have ever seen. I was sitting with my colleagues in the *Ghost Trackers* van, watching the video monitors. We saw our young investigators get intense readings on their equipment, heard strange sounds (including footsteps), and even caught a fleeting glimpse of an odd shadow that none of us could explain.

Most of the activity was centered in the small bedroom upstairs where Elizabeth had died a century-and-a-half before. Both Ghost Trackers got strong readings there, saw strange shadows, and picked up on the fact that someone had died in the room.

As it turns out, Helliwell House not only looks like the perfect haunted house, it is one too!

Ghost Tracker reading temperature changes with a digital thermometer

But what exactly do we mean when we say that a place is haunted? It seems like a simple question, but paranormal researchers don't always agree on the answer.

WHAT IS A HAUNTED HOUSE?

Haunted houses are the bread and butter of paranormal investigations. They are important, so it's helpful to understand exactly what the term means.

Some people think that a haunted house is a place where ghosts live. While that might be true to a certain extent, it doesn't really cover all the bases.

Ghost Trackers take a broader view. Since our goal is to attempt to scientifically investigate paranormal reports, we feel that any house that seems to be a landmark of unusual, unexplainable activity is worth looking into. This activity can range from strange, sudden temperature shifts,

Would You Rather...

Dracula's castle is a real place, and it's supposedly home to the ghost of Vlad the Impaler, a cruel medieval nobleman and model for Bram Stoker's legendary, blood-sucking monster. The Tower of London is also a real place and is, if the rumors are true, one of the most haunted spots on earth. Read the descriptions below, then make your choice: Would you rather spend a night in Dracula's castle or in London's infamous tower?

Dracula's castle

Dracula's haunt is a fairytale castle nestled in the mountains of Transylvania. Built in 1377 by enslaved noblemen, many of whom died during the process, it was home to the infamous Demon Prince Vlad Tepes. He had a fondness for impaling his enemies on a long spike and leaving them to die a slow, agonizing death. He was also known as Dracula (which in his language means "son of the devil"). Today, the castle is said to be haunted by dozens of Vlad's victims and by Vlad himself. A night in his castle could mean a face-to-face encounter with the "devil's son."

Tower of London

There are probably more ghosts per square foot in the Tower of London than anywhere else in the world because of the tower's long, ignoble history: over a thousand years of torture, murder, and bloody execution. The most famous ghost is the headless figure of Henry VIII's murdered wife, Anne Boleyn. For your overnight, you might stay in the Green Tower, where Anne and a host of other spirits reside. Or try the Salt Tower, where an angry poltergeist frequently attacks visitors. Don't bring your pet for protection, though. Most are too freaked out to even go in the front door.

noises with no obvious source, and reports of strong feelings of sadness and fear to unusual energy fields, objects moving on their own, and actual apparitions.

More important than the definition of "haunted house" is the question: How did the location come to be haunted in the first place?

In previous chapters, we've gone over the different theories of paranormal activity and described various kinds of apparitions. When it comes to haunted houses, many of these ideas come together. Whether you believe that paranormal activity is caused by unhappy spirits of dead people, powerful emotional forces, or some kind of unknown energy, it's clear that every haunted house has a dark secret or two to tell.

WHAT DOES SCIENCE SAY ABOUT GHOSTS AND HAUNTINGS?

Science has not been a lot of help in figuring out what haunted houses are all about. But it's not for want of trying. In fact, scientists recently performed an extensive investigation of one of the most haunted places on earth, and they left scratching their heads.

According to BBC News, a team headed by Professor Richard Wiseman carefully studied the famed Mary King's Close area in Edinburgh, Scotland's capital city. The close was an underground slum dating back four hundred years. Over the centuries, hundreds of people died in this underground slum.

Wiseman sent groups of ghost-hunting volunteers to four separate locations in the close and asked them to conduct a thorough paranormal investigation. What he didn't tell them was that only two of the locations were rumored to be haunted.

After the investigations were completed, scientists compared the volunteers' notes. The findings surprised them. There was more paranormal activity reported in the locations that already had reputations for being haunted.

In fact, in the most haunted spot – supposedly home to a sinister, black shadow ghost – 80 percent of the investigators reported finding something weird.

"Sometimes people just felt very cold," Professor Wiseman told the reporters, "but there were some quite extreme experiences – feelings of being watched, being touched, and having clothing pulled, apparitions of people and animals, and the sound of footsteps. I was surprised at the extent of the experiences."

In the two locations where there were no previous reports of haunting, paranormal researchers found some minor freaky stuff going on.

Is this proof positive that ghosts exist in the other two haunted locations? Well, the professor and crew did find some physical differences between the two kinds of sites. The "haunted" locations were much more humid than the non-haunted ones. This could explain why people felt colder in the haunted sites.

Also, there was a lot more low-frequency noise in the haunted sites. These are noises that are too low for human ears to hear, but they can still make people feel anxious and upset.

Could these factors account for the investigators' reports of paranormal activity? Not even Professor Wiseman is sure.

"It could be that ghosts were down there," he told the BBC, "but I think the explanation is primarily psychological."

Clearly, Wiseman's study does not offer any final answers. But it's a great starting point as we explore the world of ghosts, ghost-hunting, and other paranormal phenomena.

TRAGIC ENDINGS?

Most haunted houses seem to have been the scene of a tragic incident. Maybe it was a murder or suicide, or, like at Helliwell House, a sudden death or horrible accident occurred there. Sometimes, it doesn't even involve a tragic death at all. Remember the story of the Brown Lady of Raynham Hall? She lived a full life and died peacefully in her sleep. But, when alive, she had been the victim of horrible treatment by her husband, who had locked her away from her friends and family. It was her life, and not her death, that was tragic.

Other times, it seems that the building itself doesn't have to be directly connected to a tragedy, it just needs to be important to the people involved in a tragedy. The Walker Theatre in Winnipeg, Canada, is a good example. In 1913, two world-famous stage actors of the time starred in a sold-out performance of a play called *Typhoon* at the theater.

It was the last stop on a world tour for Laurence Irving and Mabel Hackney. Little did the married couple realize that it would be their last performance – ever.

The day after the performance, they took a train to Montreal. There, they boarded the *Empress of Ireland*, a passenger ship that was to take them home to their native England. However, the ship never made it to open ocean. As night fell, a thick fog descended on the famous St. Lawrence Seaway, making it very difficult for the captain and crew to see. Suddenly, there was a loud crash, and the ship lurched forward. The *Empress* had been struck by the *Storstad*, a steamship heading in to Montreal.

The *Empress of Ireland* began leaking, and within ten minutes, the ship went down, taking 1,014 passengers and crew with her.

Laurence Irving was one of the few who got away. He

The Empress of Ireland

made it safely to some rocks, but when he couldn't spot his beloved wife, Mabel, he dove back into the raging waters to find her.

Laurence and Mabel both died that night.

Years later, strange things started to happen at the theater where the couple gave their last performance. Late at night, visitors to the Walker Theatre have heard footsteps and the sound of people clapping. Even ghostly voices have been recorded on tape. Many of the people who have encountered these strange activities believe the ghosts of Laurence and Mabel have returned to the scene of their final triumph.

Is My House Haunted?

How can you tell if your house is haunted? Short of seeing an actual ghost, there are other clues. If three or more of the following descriptions apply to your home, then there is a good chance that your house might just be haunted.

1. I hear strange noises, like foot-steps, during the night or when no one else is home.

2. Something seems to be scaring my dog or cat; they refuse to go into a certain room in the house and sometimes my dog barks at something when nothing is there.

3. There are unexplained hot or cold spots in my house.

4. Sometimes I feel like someone is watching me when I know no one is there.

5. Things like lights and electrical appliances turn on and off by themselves.

6. Sometimes it feels like the bed is shaking or moving a little.

7. Sometimes, out of the corner of my eye, I see strange shadows that seem to be moving.

8. Sometimes it feels like an invisible hand is touching my arm or the back of my neck.

9. There is one room in the house that freaks me out. Whenever I go in it, I get shivers up and down my spine.

10. Things seem to mysteriously move from one place to another in the middle of the night.

THE MANIAC MANSION AND OTHER UNUSUAL HAUNTS

The Winchester Mansion in San Jose, California, built over the course of thirty-eight years, may well be one of the most haunted – and strangest – houses on earth.

The story began in the 1880s, when a woman named Sarah Winchester became convinced that spirits were targeting her. Sarah had recently been made a widow, and she had also lost her only child, baby Annie, years before that. In her grief, she began a construction project that would keep her busy for the rest of her life.

You see, Sarah had been married to a man named William Winchester, founder of the rifle company that still bears his name. When he died, he left Sarah an unbelievable fortune. Despite her wealth, she was not happy. She believed ghosts were following her around. Her worst fears were confirmed when she visited a medium, who told her that she was being haunted by the spirits of everyone who'd been killed by a Winchester rifle. So Sarah began work on a haphazard house, having it built one room at a time, and following such a jumbled pattern that the ghosts would have a hard time keeping up with her.

Construction of the Winchester Mansion began in 1884 and continued until Sarah's death in 1922. Over that period, workers completed 160 different rooms, including forty separate bedrooms.

Today, the house is a popular tourist attraction and is on every Ghost Tracker's must-see list. The mansion seems to be haunted by an entire squadron of spirits – including old Sarah herself, who, in the afterlife, has gone from being the hauntee to the haunter.

Tales of places like the Winchester Mansion bring to mind an important question. Do ghosts get to choose the places they haunt? Some researchers would say *yes*, that some ghosts, like poltergeists and crisis apparitions, do have a say in where they appear. Others believe that ghosts are really just remnants of energy – remember the Stone Tape Theory – and do not have thoughts or feelings of their own.

In either case, there are a lot of ghost stories that just don't fit the profile of a traditional haunted house.

Take the tale of Flight 401. This Eastern Airline plane crashed in the

Florida Everglades in the early 1970s, killing more than half of the passengers and crew members on board.

Afterward, the spirits of some of those who died were reportedly seen

A Bad Case of Gas

Over the years, science has been able to solve some of the mysteries associated with haunted houses. Consider the following eyewitness report. Recorded almost a hundred years ago in the *American Journal of Ophthalmology*, the case was examined by a leading scientist of the day and declared to be completely authentic.

> *On one occasion, in the middle of the morning, as I passed from the drawing room into the dining room, I was surprised to see at the further end of the dining room, coming towards me, a strange woman, dark haired and dressed in black. As I walked steadily on into the dining room to meet her, she disappeared, and in her place I saw a reflection of myself in the mirror, dressed in a light silk waist. I laughed at myself, and wondered how the lights and mirrors could have played me such a trick. This happened three different times, always with the same surprise to me and the same relief when the vision turned into myself.*

The catch? Although the eyewitness was telling the truth, what she didn't realize was that the house where she lived was haunted – by a poorly built furnace.

In this famous story, Dr. William Wilmer explored the testimonies of a certain Mr. H and his wife. After they moved into their new home, strange things started to happen. They suffered from headaches, and they seemed extremely tired and lazy all the time. Things soon got worse. They began to hear strange sounds, and it wasn't long before ghostly apparitions were appearing around the house.

Did the house have a history of murder or tragedy? Was it built on an ancient Native American burial ground? Wilmer conducted an investigation, and he soon pinpointed the exact source of the phenomena: a faulty furnace was spewing carbon monoxide into the house. In big enough doses, this gas can easily kill a person. But in smaller doses, it can cause symptoms like headaches, upset stomachs, and even hallucinations.

The H family had its furnace fixed, and the ghosts disappeared, proving two things. First, a good Ghost Tracker should always keep an open mind. Sometimes there are natural explanations for things that seem unnatural. And second, it seems a bad case of gas can create a haunted house.

on other airplanes. Most reports centered around sightings of the ghosts of the captain and his copilot. Rumor had it that parts from the wrecked aircraft were salvaged and put on other planes.

The apparitions were seen on up to thirty different aircraft, with reports coming from other pilots, crew members, and security guards. Even one of the top managers of the airline company is claimed to have spoken to one of the spirits, mistaking him for the pilot of the flight he was on.

Is it possible that the spirits of the dead could cling to pieces of the wreckage and find their way to another plane? It's a curious question, and one that still baffles researchers.

Another weird haunting concerns the famous ship the *Queen Mary*. Certainly, when it comes to a vessel with such a long and eventful history, you might expect to find a ghost or two. And the *Queen Mary* does not disappoint. Eyewitnesses have reported no less than fifty-five ghosts aboard the boat, which is now a floating hotel in Long Beach, California.

Haunted Links

Scientists in Argentina are scratching their heads over the strange goings-on in a playground in the small town of Firmat. It seems the swings have a life of their own. Even when there is no wind, the swings start to move – at first slowly. But soon they are swinging back and forth madly, as if a phantom child is playing on them. So far there is no natural explanation. To see the swings in action, type "Argentina haunted swings" into your favorite search engine.

Built in 1936, the ship regularly traveled between Europe and North America over a period of thirty years. During that time, it was home to several births and more than fifty recorded deaths.

One of those deaths involved a worker in the engine room, where he was crushed to death in the machinery. His ghost is often seen working away in blue overalls, oblivious to time passing or to the eyes of the living. Another ghost, called the White Lady, is frequently spotted dancing by herself in the main ballroom.

Perhaps the most frightening is what goes on in the swimming pool, reportedly the most haunted place on the ship. There are no records of anyone dying in or near the pool, no stories of tragic loves or losses associated with this pleasant little place. Yet, there have been dozens of sightings of ghostly bathers enjoying a midnight dip, that even leave a trail of wet footprints coming from the pool.

Oh yes, there's one more tiny detail. The pool is completely empty. It was drained of its water years ago – although that doesn't seem to slow down our supernatural swimmers.

Why has a floating hotel, formerly a famous passenger ship, attracted a group of phantoms looking for a late-night splash? On the surface, it doesn't seem to fit any of the accepted theories. So the answer is anyone's guess. But if we do solve the mystery, it might just be an important clue in understanding the true overall nature of ghosts and their haunts.

5. GET TRACKING!
Everything You Need to Begin Your Own Ghost Tracking Adventure

PICTURE THIS.

It's late at night and you are all alone in the cold darkness of Alcatraz Prison, once famous for being the toughest, most secure prison in America – in its thirty-year history as a federal prison, no one ever successfully escaped from Alcatraz. But today it is notorious for another reason. Ghost Trackers around the world celebrate it as one of the most haunted places on earth.

You begin to move forward, carefully planting your feet. You don't want to step on a loose stone and trip.

Instinctively, your hands reach to your sides to feel that your equipment is still securely in place.

Alcatraz Prison

Electromagnetic field detector. Check! Parabolic microphone. Check! Digital thermometer. Check!

This is the biggest Ghost Track of your life, and you don't want to miss a thing. You check your headset, and you hear the voice of your partner. Sitting in a secure location, she has the site map and will lead you through the prison's scariest spots. The question is: Where to start?

You could go to the shower room, where the ghost of the prison's most famous inmate, Al Capone, is said to reside. Listen carefully, and you might hear the sound of ghostly music as Capone practices his banjo.

What the well-dressed Ghost Tracker is wearing.

Block D

Or maybe Cell Block A, where numerous investigators have reported hearing sobbing and moaning. An evil spirit has even been spotted there, a ghost of a hot-headed mob hit man named Butcher. This spirit has been known to make life unpleasant for anyone who dares enter this area after dark.

Or how about the utility corridor, where decades earlier, guards gunned down three prisoners in the midst of a daring escape attempt? Today, the corridor is believed to be one of Alcatraz's most haunted areas, and investigators regularly record cold spots, phantom footsteps, and a curious clanging noise that sounds as if an inmate is banging the cell bars with a metal coffee cup.

Finally though, you settle on Cell 14D, in the prison's infamous "Hole." This was a group of four-by-eight-foot cells in the very pit of Alcatraz; damp, dank, and deadly, the Hole is where Warden James Johnson sent the toughest prisoners in an effort to break their rebellious spirits.

Hundreds of men were sent to the Hole during Alcatraz's heyday, and many of them died during the tortuous ordeal. One story concerns a man locked in the Hole who was calling for help, crying that a creature

If Ghosts Aren't Ghosts, What Are They?

Not everybody thinks ghosts are spirits of dead people that have come back to haunt the living. Today, many serious scientists are exploring ghostly phenomena to try and figure out what is going on at a scientific level. Here are some of the theories currently under investigation, as identified on The Ghost Experiment Web site at www.psy.herts.ac.uk/ghost.

Magnetism. Some Canadian researchers think that geomagnetism could be at the heart of most hauntings. These are strong magnetic fields created by natural forces, such as shifts in the earth's tectonic plates and solar flares. Scientists believe that these magnetic forces could stimulate the part of the brain that causes hallucinations.

Infrasound. Could very low-frequency sounds cause some of the phenomena we associate with haunted houses? It's a theory put forth by a professor named Vic Tandy, who came up with the idea after seeing a ghostly, gray figure appear in his workshop. The next day, another strange thing happened. Tandy noticed that one of his fencing swords was vibrating for no apparent reason. He eventually tracked the source down to a fan, which was emitting a very deep noise that human ears could not detect. Tandy was able to demonstrate that this infrasound noise caused the vibrations, and he speculated that it also could have caused his eyeball to vibrate, creating a formless, gray optical illusion.

Psychological. Some researchers think the power of suggestion plays a big role in haunting. Just knowing that there have been reports of ghostly sightings in a house, researchers claim, means that you are more likely to see and feel inexplicable things in that location.

Temperature. Strange cold and hot spots are often a feature of paranormal investigations. Some researchers believe that most of these temperature anomalies are natural, caused by the drafts in poorly insulated houses.

with glowing red eyes was attacking him. The guards could hear him screaming from inside his cell, but – thinking it was just a trick – they ignored his pleas.

The next morning, the guards found the man dead in his cell. Impossibly, he had been strangled.

But the story doesn't end there. Later that morning, when the guards did their head count, they seemed to have one prisoner too many. Over the years, lots of people had tried to sneak out of Alcatraz, but no one had ever tried to sneak in. They double-checked their math, and still it added up to one man too many.

Things got even stranger. Later that day, a new shift of guards came to work, and when they did a head count, all prisoners were present and accounted for . . . including the one who had died in the Hole the night before. When the second shift of guards was told of the prisoner's death, they were speechless. They had seen the man in the lineup that morning and had counted him in their tally.

Had his spirit come back for one last role call?

Today, the Hole continues to terrify the living. Investigators have reported a range of weird phenomena, including sudden temperature shifts, intense feelings of dread, foul smells, sounds of crashing and cell doors slamming shut, and even the odd sighting of a phantom with glowing eyes.

You take a moment to focus your attention, and then you begin the freakiest night of your life on a real-life ghost hunt through one of the scariest places you'll ever find.

That's what Ghost Tracking is all about: carefully planning, doing your research, making sure your equipment is in place, then swallowing your fear and stepping into the dark unknown.

So how do you get from here to there? Well, so far, we've had a haunted history lesson, looked at the work of scientists and paranormal researchers, learned about the different kinds of ghostly apparitions, and explored the ins and outs of haunted houses. Now it's time to put it all together.

When we train Ghost Trackers for the show, we always start with the basics. It's something we like to call the Three *E*'s: evidence, equipment, and exploration. These are the fundamental things that Ghost Trackers need to focus on to make sure they investigate a ghost or haunting in the best way possible.

What do we mean by these terms?

Evidence refers to the clues and proof that Ghost Trackers search for when investigating. Did they find any? How did they collect it? How did they analyze it? What conclusions did they draw from the evidence?

Exploration is a term we use when we want to talk about how well the Ghost Trackers explore a haunted house or location. Did they survey the entire location? Did they check everywhere, even the really scary places like a basement, attic, or tunnel? Did they keep their cool? If something really freaky happened, were they able to settle down and continue their investigation?

Equipment refers to how well Ghost Trackers use and understand their gear and tools. Did they know the names of all the equipment pieces? Were they able to operate everything easily, or did they fumble around? Did they know how to read the data?

Now, let's look at each of these fundamentals in more detail.

EVIDENCE

It would be fantastic if every Ghost Tracker investigation produced concrete proof that ghosts exist – a video of a poltergeist tap dancing across a kitchen counter, say, or a candid snapshot of you arm in arm with a smiling spirit. The reality is that Ghost Trackers have to be very patient and concentrate on collecting a wide range of evidence during an investigation. Sure, you may

Seven Simple Rules for Tracking Ghosts

Respect. Safety. Careful planning. These are the keys to a great Ghost Track. To help you get the most out of your investigation, we compiled a simple Ghost Trackers' Code of Conduct.

1. We never go Ghost Tracking alone. We always go tracking with at least one friend or we remain in direct radio contact with an expert Ghost Tracker.
2. We always check each site carefully during the daytime to plan our route and check for hazards. Safety first.
3. We never, ever trespass: we always get permission to visit a haunted site. Likewise, we always tell our parents what we are up to before we begin an investigation.
4. We never go to any site without proper equipment and appropriate clothes.
5. Fear is okay, but if we get too frightened, we leave the site. Fear makes it difficult to think clearly, and Ghost Trackers always need their wits about them.
6. We always respect our (g)hosts. We avoid sarcasm, jokes, and loud noises in haunted settings, and we never break things or damage property in any way.
7. We question everything. Only through careful research and study will we be able to unlock the mysteries of ghosts and other paranormal activities. We are scientists, exploring a whole new world.

occasionally capture an otherworldly voice on tape or even see a strange apparition that simple science cannot explain. But most of the time, it's the small things that will help you decide if a place is haunted or not.

Variety is the spice of life, they say, and it is also the key to a successful ghost hunt. There is a range of evidence you can collect when you are investigating a haunted house. Here are a few important types.

Sensations and Emotions. We use a lot of sophisticated equipment on *Ghost Trackers*, but nothing comes close to matching the power of the human mind. That's why Ghost Trackers need to be in tune with their own thoughts and feelings. Often, a strange feeling or sensation is the earliest clue that something curious is going on. Many Ghost Trackers record their thoughts and feelings during an investigation, and then they compare notes with other Trackers to see if there are any similarities. Being aware of what's going on in your mind is the first step in a great paranormal investigation.

Unusual Electrical Activity. Are you feeling electricity in the air?

Are Ghosts Becoming Extinct?

Will ghosts one day go the way of the dinosaur? Some paranormal researchers think the answer is *yes*. The reason?

Believe it or not: it's cell phones.

Tony Cornell, who's with the British Society for Psychical Research, a group that studies paranormal activity, thinks that the increase in mobile technology might be interfering with the spirit world.

"Ghost sightings have remained consistent for centuries," Cornell told reporters from the *Sunday Express*. "But with the introduction of mobile phones fifteen years ago, ghost sightings began to decline to the point where now we are receiving none."

What's going on?

Many researchers believe that ghosts and spirits exist as a kind of electrical energy. With millions of people using cell phones and other electronic devices to text, phone, and e-mail, ghosts are being overwhelmed. The ghosts are still there. It's just hard for them to compete with all the other electronic activity going on now.

But don't worry. You're not going to find ghosts on the endangered species list anytime soon. It is a good idea, though, to turn your cell phone off next time you decide to go on a late-night ghost hunt.

Is your compass moving erratically? These may be indicators of unusual or unexplainable electrical activity. It could be because ghosts give off energy. Or maybe they are made up of some strange kind of electrical force. The best thing to do if you sense weird energy is to use your electromagnetic field (EMF) detector. A high reading confirms your sensations and suggests paranormal activity.

Cold Spots and Other Temperature Anomalies. It happens all the time. During an investigation, a Ghost Tracker will feel a sudden chill or cold spot. No one knows why this happens, although some researchers believe that that kind of sensation occurs when we pass through a spirit. The best way to confirm that you have encountered a cold spot, and aren't just imagining it, is to use an infrared thermometer, a sensitive tool that can pinpoint sudden temperature changes.

EVP. Electronic Voice Phenomena is one of the most compelling kinds of evidence. These are voice sounds that are usually missed by a Ghost Tracker in the midst of an inspection. The best way to capture this kind of evidence is to set up a tape recorder at the beginning of the investigation and just let it run. Afterward, carefully listen to the tape for background voices and other sounds.

Orbs, Strange Lights, and Other Visual Clues. One of the most common kinds of evidence is orbs – mysterious balls of colored light. While Ghost Trackers occasionally spot them out of the corner of their eyes, orbs and other common light phenomena are best captured with a still or video camera.

EQUIPMENT

Knowing what kind of evidence to look for is one thing, but Ghost Trackers also need to know how to measure, monitor, and record that evidence. Back in Harry Price's day, paranormal investigators were pretty much confined to a laboratory setting when they conducted their research. Sophisticated equipment that was portable enough to take to an actual haunted location did not exist: investigators had to get by with a compass and notepad.

Today, there is a wide range of high-tech tools available to Ghost

Trackers, most of them easy to use and fairly affordable. We don't recommend you spend a fortune to equip yourself for your next ghost hunt. A basic tool kit for a safe and successful investigation consists of things you probably already have at home: flashlight, notepad, compass, portable audio recorder (tape or digital, it doesn't matter), and camera.

But for those of you who are a little more serious and have a bit of money to spend, here is a full listing of Ghost Tracking gear. You can buy most of these items at your local hardware or building supply store, while virtually all of them can be ordered online.

EMF (electromagnetic field) Detector. This simple device is one

of the most important tools for serious Ghost Trackers. It measures changes in electrical activity. The higher the reading, the greater the electrical activity. Many researchers have noticed that high energy readings often happen during paranormal activity. Ghost Trackers use the EMF detector when they sense something strange

Electromagnetic Field Detector

is going on or feel a ghostly presence.

Compass. You can use this small, simple, and inexpensive Ghost Tracking tool to get a quick and easy read on unusual electrical activity. If the arrow points anywhere but north, you know something strange is going on. It's also a practical aid if you get lost in a big house or other large area.

Still Camera. This indispensable piece of equipment can help you prepare for an investigation: take photos of the site during the day to become familiar with your environment beforehand. A still camera is also helpful during an investigation. Ghost Trackers often take lots of photos and examine them afterward for orbs, strange shadows, or ghostly faces.

What To Use — And When

Here is an easy guide that identifies the best equipment to pack for each kind of apparition.

CRISIS APPARITIONS. These ghosts usually appear to warn people of impending danger. They are unpredictable and hard to investigate. USE: Notebook, still camera, audio recorder.

ECTOPLASM. It appears as a glowing, swirling mist or as a gooey, sticky substance. Trackers often report feeling a strong energy presence, a kind of electric tingling sensation. USE: An EMF detector or Geiger counter to measure electrical activity.

ORBS, PLASMOIDS AND STREAMERS. The most common kind of phenomena. They can occur at almost any investigation. USE: A still camera. Make sure the lens is clean.

POLTERGEISTS. These troublesome spirits make their presence felt, but are rarely seen. They move objects, make loud noise, and touch people. USE: Video and audio recorders. You might even be able to detect EVP (electronic voice phenomena).

RESIDUAL HAUNTINGS. These are good to investigate since they usually appear repeatedly at the same location. USE: Video and audio recorders and an EMF detector or Geiger counter.

SHADOW GHOSTS. These thin shadows hide among other shadows and are very difficult to record. USE: Digital video cameras.

SPIRITS. They provide a great opportunity for investigators because they tend to produce a lot of evidence — sights, sounds, smells, and feelings — and are almost constantly present in a set location. USE: Your full range of tracking equipment including a digital thermometer to detect cold spots and a notepad to record feelings, sounds, and smells.

GHOST LIGHTS. These lights have no obvious point of origin. They appear over and over again in the same location. USE: A still or video camera and an EMF detector or Geiger counter.

VORTICES. These prized finds, often go unnoticed until they show up in photographs or on video. USE: Still and video cameras. Make sure that the lens is clean and that the room is relatively free of dust and insects to avoid false vortex images.

Know Your Stuff

Do you know the meaning of these common paranormal phenomena? Take this little test and match the word with its definition.

1. Clairvoyance   **a.** The belief that planets and stars can influence human events.

2. Channeling   **b.** The ability to read minds and communicate directly with other people's minds.

3. Séance   **c.** A person who can communicate with spirits.

4. Reincarnation   **d.** To write without thinking, guided by an unseen spirit.

5. Astrology   **e.** When, while you are still alive, your spirit leaves your body and travels around.

6. Extrasensory Perception (ESP)   **f.** A meeting of people who gather together to try and summon up a ghost.

7. Telepathy   **g.** When your spirit is born again in another body after you die.

8. Astral Projection   **h.** When a spirit enters a living person's body to communicate with friends and family.

9. Automatic Writing   **i.** The ability to see into the future.

10. Medium   **j.** The ability to use special senses other than seeing, hearing, tasting, feeling, and smelling.

Answer Key

1-i. 2-h. 3-f. 4-g. 5-a. 6-j. 7-b. 8-e. 9-d. 10-c.

Infrared Thermometer. This easy-to-use and inexpensive tool can pinpoint changes in temperature instantly. It's great for finding or confirming the presence of cold spots, those unusual icy areas often found in haunted houses.
Video Camera. Like a still camera, a video camera is an excellent way to both help prepare for an investigation and to carry one out. We regularly take the footage we shoot during an investigation to the Ghost Tracker lab so we can search for paranormal activity we might have missed during the investigation.
Parabolic Microphone. This powerful, directional microphone allows Ghost Trackers to focus on particular sounds. This special tool picks up sounds that the human ear might miss.
Tape Recorder/Digital Recorder. A small, hand-held one works best, allowing you to record your thoughts and feelings during an investigation. This straightforward tool also lets you check for EVP

Infrared Thermometer

Parabolic Microphone

– electronic voice phenomena – one of the most compelling kinds of evidence you can collect.

Geiger Counter. This expensive piece of equipment was originally designed to measure radiation levels. Like the EMF detector, a Geiger counter can identify unusual energy fields often associated with a haunting.

Motion Detector. This inexpensive, readily available tool can help Ghost Trackers uncover a hoax (you can catch someone sneaking around in one room while you are investigating another). Motion detectors are also easily set off by poltergeists, spirits, and other paranormal phenomena.

Motion Detector

EXPLORATION

When it comes to Ghost Tracking, evidence is the *what*, equipment is the *how*, and exploration is the *where*. You can scour a reportedly haunted location for hours, but if you don't know where to go, it could all be for nothing.

What makes for a successful exploration of a haunted house? The first step is to do your research. Every haunted house has a lot of stories associated with it. Read up on the history of the location you are going to investigate, interview people familiar with the location, and – importantly – talk to eyewitnesses who've already had a paranormal encounter there.

The next step is to visit the site during the day. Familiarize yourself with the layout and identify potential hazards (like loose boards on a creaky stairway, or odd dips and peaks in ancient floorboards). Also, pinpoint your nearest exits: sometimes, if things are getting too crazy, you might feel the need to get out of an investigation as quickly as possible. Knowing the nearest way out is essential.

Is Your TV a Window Into the Paranormal?

Your next Ghost Track may be no farther away than your TV set.

About thirty years ago, a German researcher named Klaus Schreiber was talking to some friends one night about EVP – electronic voice phenomena – when he decided to try a little experiment for fun.

He turned on his video recorder and invited the spirit of a recently deceased friend to pay a visit. He left the camera running for ten minutes and could not believe the results when he checked the camera afterward. While no image appeared, the group did clearly hear a voice. "Hello, friends," was all it said.

Schreiber began experimenting with different systems, and, in time, he developed a technique he called instrumental transcommunication (ITC). He would turn on a TV and find a channel with no signal, just static. Then he would set up a video camera fairly close to the screen, and he'd videotape several minutes of the static.

Schreiber discovered that when he reviewed the tape a frame at a time, he would find ghostly images about 50 percent of the time.

What exactly is going on? No one knows for sure. But Schreiber's technique has been tried by dozens of other researchers, many of whom have also reported positive results.

Does this mean your TV could be a portal to the unknown? Well, believe it or not, the answer just might be *yes*.

Finally, you should prepare a site map. Finding your way around a spooky, old house or building in daylight is one thing, but it's a different story altogether in the dark of night. A site map helps you find your way around after the lights are down. Draw a rough outline of each storey (for example: first floor, second floor, basement, attic) on a piece of paper, and sketch a small rectangle for each room. It's a good idea to label each room too, to mark the doorways clearly and to highlight any rooms you particularly want to investigate . . . or avoid.

Following these simple steps won't guarantee that you will find a ghost. But it will help make sure that you have a safe, fun, and thorough Ghost Tracking experience.

PUTTING IT ALL TOGETHER

Now, you've got everything you need. You know the history of ghosts and hauntings. You learned the theories and thoughts of some of the great minds who have studied spirits, apparitions, and other paranormal phenomena. You know what kinds of things to look for, where to go, what kind of equipment to use – everything.

The last question is: Are *you* ready? Can you set your fears aside and put your skills to the test? Are you prepared to do the research and take all the necessary precautions? And are you mentally prepared to run the risk of bumping into a real ghost?

If you're still nodding your head, then maybe, just maybe, you're ready to take the next step, the step from the comfort of your own world into the realm of the unknown. You have all the tools you need to become a Ghost Tracker, including the most important one: a driving curiosity and passion to investigate the paranormal.

Are ghosts for real? No one knows for sure, but you're now ready to start your journey of exploration. And who knows, maybe you will one day become the first Ghost Tracker to prove positive that ghosts, spirits, and other apparitions really do exist. But before you go… some wisdom from beyond the grave might be useful.

Whatever else, indeed, a "ghost" may be, it is probably one of the most complex phenomena in nature.

> – Frederick Myers, nineteenth century
> British writer and pioneer paranormal researcher.

INDEX

PHOTO CREDITS